TORN

By
Christine Hughes

TORN

Published by
Crushing Hearts and Black Butterfly Publishing

Cover by
Rue Volley
for
Vivid Designs

For my amazing husband,
James Hughes…

PROLOGUE

March
Buenos Aires, Argentina

James English stepped out onto the sidewalk as a chilly fall wind stung his lungs and rattled his tired bones. Pulling his coat tighter and tucking the box under his arm, he kept to the shadows of the poorly lit street but he knew that wouldn't be enough to hide from those he could feel were still watching him. Those who wanted what he had. Those who would kill to get it. Those who *had* killed trying to get it.

He devoted his life to protecting it, guarding it, and just as those who had tried in the past, the newcomer would test his limits. Without someone to keep it from falling into their hands, everything would end. The balance would shift and everything would tumble into chaos. Walking the blurred lines between good and evil wasn't an easy task. The thought shook him to his core and he hiked the box deeper into his grip and quickened his pace. A little farther and he would have time to think. He needed to think. And he couldn't do it out here. Exposed.

Suddenly, he stopped walking and cocked his ear to the night. He heard nothing but the whistling breeze rustling the leaves that still clung to the trees overhead. But he could have sworn he'd heard something else. Something indistinguishable. Something ominous.

He found me.

He began to run. It drew louder, closer. The harsh flap of wings. But his feet couldn't carry him fast enough. Not fast enough to get away from the one who had betrayed him.

This time he wouldn't make it. He knew that, had come to terms with it the moment he discovered he'd been betrayed. His was a mission that could only end in death. His death. That decision was made long ago. But now it was all happening too soon.

There were so many things he had yet to do. He needed more time. More time to prepare, to train, to lay out the truth. He'd never taken the time to explain any of it to her. He feared without his guidance, she would not understand. She would not choose the path he had wanted to groom her for. It was a hard choice for him to make and knew his headstrong daughter wouldn't embrace such a concept so easily.

But there was nothing he could do about it now. He just hoped the plan that he had laid in place would be enough. That *they* would be strong enough, good enough to protect her, to help her. He knew she was special the moment he laid eyes on her seventeen years ago. And now he would never get to watch her grow and develop the strength that lay dormant inside her. He would never be able to help her escape her demons, the demons he knew would come for her, as they came for him and those that came before.

Breathless, he veered into an alley and dropping to his knees, slipped the box behind the nearest dumpster. He quickly muttered words that only he was privy to, words that had been passed down the line from the ones who came before him, words he had hoped to pass on to her.

But he wasn't quick enough.

He felt another presence disturb the darkness behind him as the hair on the back of his neck stood on end. Despite his overcoat, a disguise meant to harbor his identity as well as block the chill, goose bumps now covered his body as he heard the intruder's footfalls echo around him and a small chuckle float towards him.

He needed to protect the box, to try to hide it away from the one who was after it.

Unintelligible words frantically spewed from his lips and his whole being shook with the power he was invoking. With a flash of light, he threw his arms to the sky. Chanting the last words of his prayer, he was struck from behind with a force that no mortal could survive. He reeled forward, barely catching himself before slamming into the frozen pavement, his wings fallen bloody beside to him.

Gasping, on his hands and knees, he slowly turned his head to look behind him. A glittering black sword protruded from his back. He could feel the blade pressing painfully against his heart. Out of the corner of his eye, his assailant finally came into view.

"Sebastian," he whispered.

"James," Sebastian smirked.

He should have known. Once they knew the exact location of James and the box, retrieving it was a task that only Sebastian would handle himself. He should have been more careful.

"You had to know I would find you, James," Sebastian's said softly.

James quickly uttered a prayer for his daughter. A petition, asking, begging, that she would be the balance promised so many years before. He hoped it would be enough. As the sword slowly pierced James' heart, and the last glimmer of life dimmed from his eyes, he sadly realized that his incantation to send the box away may not have been successful.

Pulling his sword from James' chest, Sebastian walked over to the dumpster, shoving it across the alley with a mere wave of his hand. As he retrieved the box, a sadistic smile played on his face, victory sparked in his pale green eyes and he knew that the first half of his mission was complete.

Chapter 1

September
The Cabin

Run, Samantha. Don't look back. Just run.

I repeated this mantra over and over again as I sprinted through the trees. Focused, like my life depended on it and knowing that one day it would, I ran. Through the damp woods, past branches that tore at my skin, and hurdling over logs, I ran. My breath mingled with the crisp fall air but I didn't feel the cold. I felt nothing but the pure and relentless adrenaline that pumped through my veins. As the sun rose and cast its broken beams through the trees, I ran. With only a single thought: *I have to get there.*

I knew he was following me. He was close. So close. I couldn't let him catch me.

My legs carried me over slick moss and rotting bark. I flew over downed trees, grabbing for branches to help me over. I was fast. Faster than before. Faster than yesterday. My focus was singular. The task at hand was all I could think about. ***Get through, Sam. Faster, Sam. Jump, Sam.***

I swore I could navigate those woods with my eyes closed. I could see the next obstacle that lay ahead of me yards before it came into view. And when I concentrated hard enough, those obstacles began to disappear.

I burst into the clearing and could faintly make out his barely labored breathing behind me. He was so close I could smell him. I dug in and pumped my legs faster. Always faster. I knew I was going to beat him this time. I had to. I closed in on my destination. All I had to do was jump. I had to make it over the water. Over the creek on the other side of the clearing.

Samannnnnnthaaaa…. Run!

The intrusive voice pulsed through me and drowned out the mantra in my head, breaking my rhythm and I stumbled over a rock I was sure hadn't been there yesterday.

Damn it! The eerily familiar voice that had settled comfortably in my head like a squatter had the worst timing. It teased like a schoolyard bully and I wanted to scream. But I couldn't. I had to run. I was almost there. *Come on, Sam.* Fifty feet. Forty feet. Thirty feet. Almost there. As I braced my body for the jump over the swollen creek, he caught my ankles in mid-air and dropped me to the ground with a bone jarring tackle onto the muddy bank.

2

"Son of a bitch," I growled.

I fought back, jumping up the way I was taught, fists at the ready. I caught him off guard, for the first time, with a jab to the chin and a roundhouse to the stomach. Then I did a back spring, landing well out of his reach and quickly regrouped. The grin on his face as he rubbed his chin told me I surprised him with that one. And now I was in trouble.

"Lucky shot, Sam. Nice kick. Too bad this one's on me." His cocky bravado triggered an extra jolt of adrenaline inside me. He's not gonna take this round. Not this time.

For a few seconds we circled each other, anticipating the other's next move. He crouched and lunged at my knees. I jumped to grab the branch above me and he missed, sprawling out in the dirt. But not for long. He was on his feet again before I'd even let go of the tree, his eyes merely blue slits of predatory focus. I had a total of three seconds to figure out my next move before he lunged again, targeting me mid-waist.

Instinctively, I dropped to the ground, and sprung forward, drilling him into the trunk of the nearest tree. Rain had started to fall, shrouding the sound of my movements as I quickly disappeared behind the brush. I needed to work out how to nail him with an element of surprise.

3

He growled in frustration but his annoyance didn't matter. I was winning. I could feel it.

My hands and knees were scraped and dirty. My hair was a tangled mess and the sudden rise in humidity brought on by the rain wasn't helping. The scent of decaying vegetation around me did nothing to mask the stench of my sweat.

His voice taunted me. "Come out, come out wherever you are. You can't hide from me forever. You think you can camouflage yourself from me? I can smell you."

Think, Samantha.

He was right. I couldn't sit there all day getting soaked in the rain waiting for him to find me. Through a small gap between the leaves, I could see him looking, scanning the trees and underbrush. Then his eyes focused where I crouched. I needed to act, now.

The forces of nature seemed to heed my need for action and the sky erupted, complete with booming thunder and darting strikes of lightning. I belly crawled behind bushes until I was on his right. His eyes still boring into the spot I'd just vacated, he took a step forward.

I slowly stood and crept up next to him. He turned around and I caught his cheek with a right hook but he grabbed my hair and yanked my head back. I yelled, in surprise and pain. The look on his face made him almost unrecognizable and for a moment I was paralyzed as the maniacal voice stole through me once again.

Samannnnnnthaaaa… Run!

He took advantage of my shock and swept my legs out, dropping me face first into a vat of mud.

So not how I had envisioned this ending.

Lying face down in the muck, I struggled for breath as the weight of him held me still and his annoyingly even breath tickled my neck. I swore it was as if he had the lung capacity of a freaking whale. I could picture his grin and it made me want to punch him even more. As I turned my head away from the mud, I closed my eyes. My adrenaline spent, all the tension left my body in defeat.

"Seriously, do you have to play Monday Night Football *every time* we train? I can't wait until it's my turn to play predator. I'm so gonna drop your sorry ass in the thickest patch of poison ivy I can find. No. Sumac. Poison sumac. That sounds much worse."

Laughing, Ethan shifted his body so I could roll over. Still braced on his elbows above me, he inched up so we were eye to eye. My breath hitched.

I used to be amazed at how he could morph into the scary predator so easily. It wasn't something I could do, at least not yet. But as each day passed and the longer we waited, the more shadows I cast and the more off my rocker I became.

"I'll believe it when I see it, slowpoke. I'll be sure to run at low speed tomorrow to make life easier on you."

Jerk. I was lying there, thinking of nothing but the way the contours of his body fit nicely with mine, envisioning him kissing me in that long slow way they do in movies, and all he could do was wax sarcastic. I had to look away or, I swore, my lips were gonna pucker up on their own and plant a juicy one on his full lips.

Wouldn't that be nice?

"Tomorrow's not your day. So you can run at whatever speed you like. I won't be chasing you."

I playfully punched his arm as he gently brushed the hair from my eyes and put his forehead to mine. His eyes searched mine as his fingers grazed the side of my face.

"Your eyes are darker."

"Darker than what?" *He noticed my eyes?*

"They're still blue, just darker. I don't know."

"Well, thanks, I guess."

He smiled at me and once again thoughts of long, slow kisses filled my head.

As he tucked a strand of muddy hair behind my ears, he whispered, "You know, Sam, now that we're alone, there's something I've been meaning to tell you."

I forced boredom into my voice. "Oh yeah? What's that?" Rolling my eyes, I tried my best to act calm, while my heart threatened to beat out of my chest and *Ohmygod, ohmygod, ohmygod* ran on continuous loop through my head.

A sexy smirk played at his mouth before he leaned down to my ear. "You really, really need a shower."

I punched him again, this time with all my leftover strength. "Ethan, you suck."

Samannnnnnthaaaa...Run!

My body froze. Goosebumps littered my arms and cold fear knotted my stomach. I felt the same sudden dizziness that always came when the voice taunted me. I lifted my head and searched the woods, knowing full well I wouldn't find what I sought. The voice was everywhere and nowhere. It was familiar and foreign and creepy but mostly, it was really freaking annoying.

Ethan once told me if I focused, I could eradicate the voice. If I could just focus long enough, I could shut it up for good. All I wanted was for it to leave me alone. The voice could tell me to run all it wanted, upping the terror level every time, but since I didn't know what the hell I was supposed to be running from, it was all pointless. Pointless and terrifying.

Alarmed, Ethan stood up and scanned the woods. "What is it, Sam?"

"I heard it again. Just now. And it followed me through the woods while I was running earlier."

"We'd better get back." He extended his hand to help me up. The glint in his ocean blue eyes was familiar, but the usual knowing smirk on his face had been replaced by tension. His hair, the color of beach sand at dawn, still looked fresh. I swore he pilfered good hair genes from the pages of the latest celebrity rag. And why was it that men could still look amazing all sweaty and dirty? How was *that* fair? Lapsing into a daze, I realized too late that he was fully aware of me staring at his chest. How the white t-shirt clung just so to his nicely defined…*Shake it off.*

"Oh, by the way, dishes are on you, tonight," Ethan laughed.

"Shut up." I grabbed his hand and pulled myself to my feet. I pushed my hair out of my face and sighed as I noticed my long blonde waves had become a hideous shade of drab. Great. The mud had caked it into dreadlock-like tendrils, elegantly adorned with   dried leaves and twigs. Fashionable. Call me Mother-freaking Nature.

Doing my best to look halfway presentable, I attempted to remove the ooze from my eyes with a clumsy two fingered fling, as much for vanity's sake as for sight. But I simply swept the muck into my ears instead. *Typical.*

Ethan rubbed the welt forming on his chin. "A few of those punches were solid. Did Lucas teach you that roundhouse? And good job using the brush as camouflage."

"Yeah, I can feel myself getting stronger, faster too. But I'm just not strong enough and nowhere near fast enough yet. Just when I think I've got you, ugh, you come out of the blue and knock me on my ass."

"Well, you were closer this time. I almost didn't get you."

"Yeah, but you did. You always do. You both always do," I retorted. I knew I sounded way more like a spoiled brat than I meant to, but *damn it*, it was so frustrating.

I could feel the mud beginning to crust on my palms. I briefly contemplated smearing them all over Ethan's face as payback, but settled for wiping them on my thighs. My favorite sweatpants were now ripped and dirty anyway. I sighed. My white tank had faired no better. It was now an awesome shade of forest floor and clung to my chest like a second skin. I was sure every runway model would be sporting this look come spring. Not like it mattered what I looked like anyway. He didn't look at me the same way I looked at him.

"You know, I'd like to strangle the guy who had the brilliant idea of training at dawn."

Chuckling, Ethan turned to head toward the cabin. "I'll be sure to let Lucas know that you're gonna lobby for more sleep in the future. I'm impressed, though, with today's training." He stopped and untangled a twig from the rat's nest my hair had become. "But for now, we need to go."

"Impressive, huh? My hair full of leaves and my face full of mud? How attractive," I said, rolling my eyes.

He leaned in and touched my chin. "You'd be attractive with a shaved head and antlers growing from your ears." He straightened and I could feel my face grow warm, yet again. Well, at least he wouldn't notice with layers of mud masking my face.

"But then again, that's sort of a gross thought since you're kinda like the little sister I never had."

I struggled to hide my disappointment as I said, "Little sister?"

"Well, I meant 'little' as in vertically challenged."

I drew myself up to my full five foot four inch height but sighed as I remembered he had a foot on me. I slumped my shoulders again. Too tired for good posture and a snappy comeback, I said, "Whatever, Ethan. You suck."

"You already said that."

"Well, it needed to be said twice."

"Then by all means…"

"Are we done here? This training has kicked my ass and as you said, I'm in desperate need of a shower."

"Ah, yes. Yes, you are." He chuckled and reached for my hand. "Come on, then. We'll try again another time."

As we trudged back through the woods, I fell behind him, wanting to sneak a whiff of my pits. He was right. I seriously needed a shower. A long, hot shower.

Why did he always have to see me at my worst?

He may have been my best friend's brother but I wasn't dead. My heart raced into my throat every time he touched me, to the point I had to struggle not to faint from the closeness. Secretly, I inhaled the smell of him. *God, even his sweat smells good.* I couldn't help but stare at his back and with a small smile, I gripped his hand tighter.

He suddenly dropped to one knee, slipping his hand from mine to tie a rogue shoelace. I clenched my hand into a fist, wanting to hold onto the warmth that still lingered on my palm.

Samannnnnnthaaaa....Run!

Frozen, I scanned the trees surrounding us. I tuned my ears and tried to focus but the voice always disoriented me. My head felt still and off-balance all at once. Not only was it harassing me more frequently but it sounded closer than ever. "Ethan?" I whispered his name for reassurance.

My lack of movement seemed to jar him. "What's wrong? Did you hear it again?" he asked, eyes narrowed. He looked off into the distance trying to sense what only I could.

I nodded. "Yes," I said, my voice rising with panic.

"Damn it," Ethan whispered. "It shouldn't be able to follow you here."

Before I could ask what he meant, he shot me a half-smile that didn't quite reach his eyes and said, "Let's go, Sam. We really need to get back to the house. Like now." A sense of urgency filled the space around us. He grabbed my hand and ran, pulling me back through the woods toward the cabin. The inherent silence to which I'd grown accustomed enveloped us, so that all we heard was the sound of our footsteps. Ethan ran, repeatedly glancing at the sky and the surrounding trees, like he was bracing for what might come hurdling at us.

Chapter 2

We didn't stop running until we burst into the clearing that spread out around the cabin like a welcome mat. The last fifty yards or so seemed to take forever, like we were on a slow-moving conveyor belt. My body ached in places it didn't a few hours ago and mud had crusted over my skin. Every movement made the hair on my arms rip out by the roots, reminding me of a documentary I once saw about the mud people from Woodstock. But those people had covered themselves in mud on purpose. I shuddered at the thought of intentionally wallowing in mud like a pig and longed for a shower and the lightly scented lavender soap that would make me feel like a girl again.

It was hard to feel like one sometimes when my roommates were two guys. The two guys my dad had entrusted to care for me after he died. Two guys who always saw me as nothing more than a sibling. And barely female. Secluded in the woods, with no one to dress up for, I usually relegated myself to jeans, sweats, tanks, and sweatshirts. Long gone were the days when I would actually blow dry my hair, slick on some lip-gloss, and rock some amazing heels. But now, due to a depressing lack of social life since we moved here, I no longer saw the point.

We'd been living at my dad's old cabin for five months. Hiding, training, always training, for an ever-present danger that had yet to reveal itself. The two-story log hideout was built to be strong and yet was still beautiful. I felt all at once peaceful and safe at just the sight of it.

The ornately carved front door looked fragile with age though it was the strongest, thickest slab of wood I'd ever seen and I couldn't imagine anything getting through it. The crudely made window boxes bloomed even now with cheerful flowers, though I knew for a fact none of us had a green thumb.

I climbed the steps to the wrap around porch, the old wood creaking under my weight, and stood at the railing watching the surrounding woods. The porch had become my haven for meditation. Enveloped by woods and wildlife, I loved it there. I was never a nature girl, but this place, my father's cabin, was an exception. The trees were always full and lush, standing guard over us, watching us. And I felt safe.

I dared the voice to manifest itself, only feeling braver now that the familiar log structure stood behind me, supporting me.

As I reached for the worn door handle that seemed so pathetic against the impressive door, Ethan stopped me. "Try not to worry about the voice. You should just go in, shower and rest. You look beat."

I was sure he meant to say *you look like hell*, but I brushed it off. The mud on my face cracked as I forced a smile and told him, "I'm fine."

"You're not fine, Samantha."

"Yes, I am. It's just a voice, Ethan, and it's not like this is the first time I've heard it. And probably not the last."

"Right, it's just a voice. A voice that follows you day and night. A voice that comes out of nowhere and everywhere at once. Look, just promise me you'll get some rest and relax a bit before you collapse."

"Fine," I said, rolling my eyes. "I promise." Lying always made me feel like crap and I tried not to squirm but he was asking for the impossible. Well, it wasn't *exactly* a lie anyway. I knew I would rest and relax if I could ever figure any of this out, but how did he expect me to tune out a noise when I wasn't even sure of the source. And it wasn't like I could just pop earplugs in and pass out. "Okay? Can I go shower now?"

He looked as though he wanted to say something more but instead grabbed my hand and squeezed it tightly. I looked away, hoping he hadn't seen the stupid smile on my face and pulled the front door open.

We walked into the house and Ethan instantly released my hand. His brother, Lucas, stood in the kitchen waiting for us and eating a bowl of something. Knowing Lucas it was likely some sort of healthy granola crap. I suddenly craved sugar. Lots and lots of sugar.

He was wearing nothing but a pair of old, ratty low-slung jeans, his slouching posture doing nothing to diminish his amazing abs. Apparently the healthy granola crap was working. His favorite band blasted from the portable iPod dock on the counter.

He looked up as we entered the kitchen. "What's up, guys?"

Ethan smiled at me then danced over to the iPod dock, turning up the volume. *Yooooou... Your sex is on fire...* "Man, I love this song."

"You would. Perv." But, of course, my foot started tapping to the catchy beat.

"Aw, Sam. You love me."

"Shut up, *Ace*." I loved using the nickname he would never allow anyone else to use, just to piss him off. It was a subtle reference to the fact that, even though most people believe him to be a dumb jock, he still scored perfectly on his SAT's. Lucas and I were the only ones that knew though as he'd refused to

18

share that information with anyone except us. He seemed embarrassed to be smart, not just smart-ass smart, but smart-smart.

A familiar but uncomfortable warmth rose within me and my skin tingled as I realized I was staring at him like an idiot. His impromptu dance momentarily made me want to slip him a dollar. Needing to focus on something else, I averted my eyes, but not before Ethan noticed. His chiseled face broke into a knowing grin. I could swear he always knew what I was thinking. These feelings were totally off limits because even though he wasn't my brother, he might as well be.

As far back as I could remember Lucas and Ethan had always been there. It was like they were the only people in my past who'd ever existed, especially after my dad died. Ethan, as my best friend's brother, was totally off limits to the funny stomach churning that arrived whenever I saw him. He has always been the *I-wish-he-would-look-at-me-the-way-I-want-him-to* guy.

Lucas, on the other hand, had tightened up a bit from his days of practical jokes and boisterous laughter. He's flip-flopped sporadically between the old Lucas and the new moody, often confusing and unusually suspicious Lucas. We'd been best friends since I could remember, but over ever since his dad died he'd distanced himself from me. Every time I tried to talk to him about it he'd change the subject or blow me off. My heart broke a little more whenever I pondered this slow, bizarre change in him and I couldn't help wondering if it was something I did. He was supposed to be my rock after my dad died but now that job fell to Ethan.

Lucas dropped his cereal bowl into the sink. Crossing his arms over his bare chest he said, "How'd she do?"

Ethan stripped off his shirt and used it to wipe the sweat from his face. "She did just fine. She's getting faster. Right, Sam?"

"Uh, umm," I stammered. Ethan's sweaty, naked chest was distracting me and I was a little embarrassed at the thoughts going through my head. "I did ok. I was almost able to jump the creek today. I get closer with each training session but I always fall short. Then we went at it with a little hand to hand and I was winning too until the voice interrupted."

Concerned, Lucas asked, "Again with the voice? Then what happened?"

I laughed nervously. "What happened? He proceeded to tackle me face first into the mud, as you can see. That's what happened. It's great, actually. I have my very own spa facial in the woods. I'm sure I could bottle it and run Clearasil out of business. But thanks for asking."

Great, I was sounding like a brat again. With a huff, I walked into the living room and fell into the couch, not caring that it would have to be steam cleaned to get the dirt off or that I would be the one doing it. I smeared a little into the cushion with my palm for good measure as I tried to shrink further into myself.

"*I'll* practice with you tomorrow, Sam. I'll show you how to avoid getting tackled."

"But Lucas, I'm sure she doesn't mind…"

"Shut up, Ethan!"

Ethan ignored his brother. "Aw, Sam. It just takes practice. We've only been training for six months. You'll get the hang of it. You just have to remember how…"

"It isn't about being tackled. Don't you get that?" I retorted as anger bubbled up from nowhere. "When are we going to quit wasting time with training and actually deal with the real problems? What am I even training for? Who am I supposed to be fighting? Why can't anyone find Sebastian? Is it his voice I keep hearing?

"It's been six months already, for Christ's sake! And what makes you think Sebastian come after me? And if he does, what makes you believe I'll ever be strong enough to fight him off?"

I sighed. So many questions, yet not one of them had an answer. It was the same fight over and over again and I was tired of it. From their slumped shoulders and glazed expressions, I apparently wasn't the only one either. So many times I wished I could just go home. Back to my senior year of high school, back to my house, back to the peaceful days before my dad died. But Lucas and Ethan always danced around that topic. With them, it was always training, training, and more training.

"...as you know. We are doing this for your own good....

I closed my eyes, barely listening as Lucas rattled off the same line he always gave me. God, I was so tired.

Chapter 3

March
{Pensacola, Florida}

I walk into the house and toss my backpack, as per usual, on the couch. *Should I get a head start on that report of* <u>Slaughterhouse Five</u> *that's due for English class or should I just go for a swim? It was an unusually warm day.* Decisions, decisions. I honestly don't feel like doing much of anything. Deciding to make myself a little snack while I contemplate my options, I pop in my ear buds and saunter into the kitchen.

Jamming to my newest playlist, I vaguely hear the doorbell ring. Irritated at the interruption to my potentially life altering decision-making process, I spin around and stalk to the front door.

Opening the door, I find no one there. It isn't until I step out onto the porch that I almost stumble over it. A package with my name on it. No address, just my name in flowing gold letters. I scan the street looking for evidence of who would have left it. Bending down to pick it up, I realize I would definitely need two hands. It isn't very big but surprisingly heavy. I heft it into the house, close the door with my foot and scream.

"Jesus Christ, Ethan. You scared the crap out of me!"

Doubled over as if in pain, Ethan laughs. "You should've seen your face. Priceless!"

"Ha, ha. I'm so glad you find my personal terror so hilarious." I then notice he's wearing the new swimming trunks we'd bought at the mall the other day. Decision made. *Later, Vonnegut.*

Walking into the dining room, I say, "Let me put this down and I'll go put on my bathing suit."

I hurry upstairs and throw on my new blue Roxy bikini. After a quick leg rub to check for stubble, I sniff my pits and twist my hair into a knot. Ethan had once mentioned he liked it that way.

Stop it, Samantha. He doesn't like you that way. My eyes roll and I'm convinced my subconscious is trying to bully me into thinking there's no chance with him, but can't blame a girl for trying.

Slathering on my SPF 30, I grab my towel and head back downstairs. I pause at the bottom step when I suddenly hear two murmuring voices coming from the kitchen. I smile when I realize Lucas is here. All conversations stop, however, when I walk into the room and find just about every snack in the pantry strewn across the countertop. I notice the box has been moved from the dining room table to the kitchen counter.

"What's up, guys?" I really hate it when people stop talking just as I walk into a room.

With an approving eye, Ethan answers, "Nothing much, Sam. Nice bathing suit. Really shows off your ears."

Feeling uncomfortably flushed, I wrack my brain for something clever to say but all I manage to squeak out is, "Err, uh. Thanks. You too."

Ethan just laughs and I want to punch him. He always gets me tongue-tied and he knows it. How is it that I can just be myself around Lucas but whenever his brother is around I literally lose the ability to act like a human being?

"Hey Sam," Lucas questions. His casual tone sounds forced. "What's in the box?"

"I don't know. It just showed up on the doorstep. I was bringing it in when Ethan decided to play 'let's scare the hell out of Sam'." I stick my tongue out at Ethan before turning back to Lucas. "I don't even know who it's from."

Ethan pipes in, "Aren't you curious? No return address, just your name on some brown paper package? Looks like someone's got a secret admirer."

"Ha. Funny. As a matter of fact, I was going to open it." I run my fingers over the paper wrapping. "The handwriting is pretty, isn't it? I like how it looks as though my name just floats above it. The flowery script reminds me of something, but I can't place it." Mesmerized by its simplicity, I stare a beat too long at the package before I shake a load of cobwebs from my head.

"Earth to Sam." Snapping his fingers in my face, Ethan pulls me back to reality.

"Uh, let me get something to open this. I don't want to damage the paper."

Lucas and Ethan exchange a glance that I can't quite read and I grab a knife from the drawer, delicately slicing through the tape. Once the paper is off, I fold it so my name won't be wrinkled. Maybe I can put it in my scrapbook later. It's just so pretty.

Under the paper is a cardboard box. In the same ethereal script are weird symbols I don't recognize. "What does that…"?

"Hope." Lucas answers before I finish my question.

"Hope? As in, uh, just hope?" Sometimes I can't control the brainiac inside.

Ethan looks over, his blue eyes strangely dark. "It's the Greek word for Hope."

"How on earth would you know? You barely passed Spanish."

"I'm smarter than the average bear," Ethan says with a wink. "Open the box."

"That's odd. Why would someone send me a package that says hope on it?"

"Just open the box, Sam," Lucas whispers impatiently.

Lucas is never impatient. Moody, yes. Impatient, no. I stare at him for a moment, confused. Am I seeing the beginning of a whole new side to him? I'm not sure I like it. With his fingers tapping on the countertop and eyes glued to the box, he looks edgy, a bit worried.

Ethan, on the other hand, is calmly leaning against the counter, his arms crossed. If I didn't know better, I'd think he was disinterested but he isn't. I can see it. Both of them are white-knuckled and tense.

"Fine," I whisper back, trying to keep the unexpected and sudden dread from growing in my voice.

Using the same knife I used to cut the paper, I carefully cut the tape holding the cardboard box closed, again trying not to mar the beautiful script that suddenly, like the words on the paper, begin to float. Peeking inside, I find an ornately carved wooden box about half the size of a shoebox. Knife still in hand, I

27

gently lift it from its packaging and set it on the counter.

"Ouch! Shit!" The knife nicks the palm of my hand and blood drips onto the lid, flowing into the intricately cut design.

Lucas moves around the counter so fast, I can't comprehend how he's suddenly next to me. As Lucas bandages my hand with a bizarre rainbow colored scarf that he pulled out of nowhere, Ethan picks up the box and carries it in front of him like a bomb to the dining room table. Everything begins to slow down and I feel disoriented. Ethan turns back to me from across the room, searching for something.

"Are you okay, Sam?" Lucas keeps asking.

"No, no. I'm fine. Really." As soon as words of protest escape my lips, the world suddenly starts to spin. My vision hazes and I reach out for the counter to steady myself. "Really, I'm fine." I barely make out Ethan yelling my name before I fall to the floor in a crumpled heap.

Their voices fade into the background as visions cloud my head. Something resembling shafts of light twirl angrily off in the distance. Darkness wraps itself around me as wind whips my hair into knotted layers. I'm somewhere unfamiliar, perched on some mountainous cliff with the sea crashing furiously below. I bring my hand slowly in front of my face and everything looks as if I'm seeing it through oily water.

Smeared and unclear, everything about this place fills me with dread and unease. Despair and hopelessness permeated the air around me, as though happiness never existed. I can't help but feel sad and confused. Seeing no way out, something inside me suddenly breaks and I feel like a cornered animal. I shiver and instinctively wrap my arms around myself.

Searching for anything familiar, my gaze is drawn toward those intense shafts of light in the distance. They seem to be getting closer. I hear the crash of the waves accompanied by a low humming sound. With each passing second the sound gets louder, filling my head. I cover my ears with my hands, trying in vain to silence the noise. Sadness drapes over me, suffocating me like an itchy wool blanket.

Then suddenly I see my dad. But it doesn't look like my dad. Not totally. Weird dark light is surrounding him and he's dressed in a long black coat I don't recognize, blending in amongst the shadows.

"Dad?" I reach out, grasping nothing and he smiles softly.

"Samantha, honey, it's your turn now."

"My turn for what?"

The sadness wears me down and small tears fall down my cheeks as he looks at me with sad, narrowed eyes. "Just remember to follow your instincts and you'll be fine. I'll be here when you need me. You have a long road ahead and you have important choices to make."

"Be where? What is this place? Where're you going? What choices?" He starts to fade further into the shadows. "No! Don't leave me!" I sob.

The wind picks up furiously and the low hum morphs into a full-blown ear-deafening buzz. It's all around me and he has to yell for me to hear him over the din. "You can't stay, Sam. You aren't ready. You have to go for now. It's in your hands. It's your turn. You have guardians to help you but trust them cautiously. You need to go now. I'll do what I can from here but you need to be ready. You're running out of time. Follow the light that burns inside you."

I watch as he takes to the sky in a sudden burst of light, swirling feathers drifting to the ground in his wake. In his place, suspended in mid-air is the most beautiful creature I have ever seen. Abruptly the commotion ceases and I am filled with an eerie calm. The wind dies down and the sea doesn't look quite so angry. Her body glows golden beneath an almost transparent dress and her wings, the color of a glittering, muted rainbow, look impossibly soft. With sad, determined eyes fixed on me, she speaks in the softest whisper and I have to strain to hear her.

"Samantha, it is time to face your fate. We need your help."

"Help with what?" I try to focus on her but the shafts of light in the distance begin to take on color and my concentration hazes. The shimmering black and gold streams look as though they are tangled in some violent dance in the heavens.

"Focus, Samantha," she whispers more sternly. "We need your help. In time you will know what to do, but for now you must hurry."

"What're you talking about? What do I have to do? Where's my dad?" My breath hitches as I try not to hyperventilate.

"Your father was a good man, Samantha. He was very proud of you. And now, he has passed the journey onto you. You must keep his memory within you. You must not let anyone make you believe he was anything but a good man."

"I still don't know what you're talking about! Tell me what you mean! Where's my dad? Please!"

"I must go now, Samantha. All will be explained in due time. You must complete your training. Be vigilant of everything and everyone. You will teeter on the edge of darkness and you will be betrayed before you can succeed. Always remember

31

that your choices will determine the fate of both hope and despair."

Before I can speak again, the beautiful winged girl disappears. The shafts of light move ever closer and darkness slowly rolls back in, filling the space around them. The sea screams out in pain as it resumes throwing itself against the jagged rocks below. Goosebumps litter my arms and beads of sweat slip over my skin as pure terror grips me. The buzzing resumes and grows louder, closer. My vision blurs as huge swarms of mutated, winged beasts with long dagger-like stingers surround me and I swat at my clothes, my hair, and my face to get them away. The noise is deafening and I feel it coming up from inside me. I can't hear myself think. I know I have to go, to leave this place, but my feet feel rooted to the ground, like hands are holding me firm, not allowing me to move.

"Sam, wake up."

I hear someone familiar whisper my name and I know I need to follow it to get out of here. I strain to listen to it over the noise, hoping to determine from which direction it is coming but panic rises inside me when I can't find it. The cliff begins to crumble a bit as though it wants to drop me into the water below. I need to focus.

I hear the voice again and realize it belongs to Lucas. I have to get to him. Turning away from the unknown and the darkness, I begin to run.

I hear his voice quiver. "Ethan, she's not waking up."

The faster I run from the cliff's edge, the harder the wind blows against me, and the louder the noise gets, the colder I feel. If I can just get to Lucas, I know he will help me but even though I'm sprinting, I don't seem to be moving forward.

Hands shake me gently, and something cool and soft is laid on my forehead. "Sam," Lucas whispers. "Please wake up."

When I look up, I see Lucas floating in the turbulent sky above me, holding out his hand. I jump to grab it and everything shuts off.

Complete darkness descends and I drift, weightless. I can still feel Lucas' hand in mine, guiding me. My body settles onto something cool and flat my eyes flutter open. My vision clears and I see Lucas staring down at me, his eyes worried. Behind him, Ethan is chewing on a fingernail and talking on the phone. I struggle to sit up.

"What happened?" I can barely manage a whisper.

"Sam! You're awake!" Lucas grabs me and pulls me into a tight hug. "Oh, thank God. You scared us."

I see the worry etched on his face. "I'm fine, I think." My head feels heavy and I reach back to touch it. "I must've hit my head. How long was I out? I had the weirdest dream."

Lucas smoothes back my hair. "Only a few minutes. You did hit your head, but not too hard. You cut your palm on the knife and must've fainted from the blood."

A few minutes? It feels like I've been gone for hours. Why does it sound like he's trying to convince himself? And why is Ethan on the phone? And since when do I pass out from a small cut and a few drops of blood?

Lucas helps me lean back against the cabinets. He hands me a glass of water and I take a sip, noticing the tremors in my hands. I untie the scarf he'd wrapped around my hand and check out the damage; it must've been one hell of a cut for me to pass out like that. But when I uncover my hand to inspect it, my mouth goes dry. The cut, the blood… has disappeared. Healed over.

Still staring at my now uninjured palm, I try to reassure them, and myself. "I'm okay, really. But that dream… it was so weird. Almost like a vision or something. I saw my dad and he told me something about it being 'my turn'. But I didn't understand what he meant."

I look up to see darkness fall over Lucas' face. The phone has slipped from Ethan's grasp and as it clatters to the floor, I jolt upright in bed, my pajamas soaking with sweat.

***

It took awhile for me to fall back to sleep. I changed into fresh pajamas, even remade the bed, but my nerves wouldn't calm down. My mind was convinced that the events in the dream were real. But when I looked for my bathing suit, I found it right where I had left it yesterday, the tags still attached.

When I awoke the next morning, Ethan was curled up into a ball on my chair. I smiled. He always seemed to know when I might need him and his presence warmed me to my toes. With my dad out of the country on yet another volunteer mission, it was comforting to know someone was there, watching over me while I slept. Laying a blanket over him, I checked the clock on my nightstand. Four in the morning was definitely too early for me to be conscious but there was no way I'd be able to get back to sleep for the second time. I could still feel the heaviness of my dream draped across my shoulders.

I stepped out into the hallway, hoping to escape the images that still lingered in my mind, haunting me. I really wanted to talk to my dad, tell him about the strange dream I'd had, but I knew it'd just make him worry and he'd insist on cutting his work short and coming home. Seeing the light on in the boys' bedroom, I walked over and knocked lightly.

Lucas opened the door quickly. "Sam? What're you doing up?"

"Couldn't sleep and didn't want to wake Ethan. What're *you* doing up?"

"The same. I woke up when Ethan left the room." He seemed to want to say more but didn't.

What was going on with him lately? It was obvious by the way he reacted that something about the change in Ethan's and my relationship bothered him, but he would never tell me what. His reluctance to speak up was more annoying than anything. It wasn't like there was anything going on between us anyway, and even if there were, I would expect a best friend to support me.

"What's with you and Ethan lately?" I asked.

"What do you mean?"

"You know what I mean. You act so weird all the time anymore. How come you didn't take up the chair in my room instead of him."

36

Impatience twisted in his face. "Look, I don't have time for this. Are you okay? Do you need anything?"

There it was again. He was pushing me away. "I'm fine. I don't need anything. You're obviously very busy doing whatever you do at four in the morning." As I turned on my heel to stalk back to my room, Lucas grabbed my arm and spun me around. I swore, for a second, I saw anger flash in his eyes before his face softened.

"Don't be mad. I'm sorry. I'm just worried about you and tired and…" He sighed. "I don't know what else." Any annoyance I felt dissipated and I reached up to hug him. "Why don't you come in and listen to music? I've been downloading songs all night. I couldn't think of anything else to do. Got some great songs. I downloaded some grunge, classic rock, even some new stuff I think you'll like!"

His enthusiasm was contagious and despite the emptiness I felt around me, I smiled back. I needed to do something to get my mind off of that dream and the chaos I could feel quietly brewing around me.

Before I knew it, it was time for us to get ready for school. I popped into my room, got dressed and raced downstairs to wait for Lucas. Ethan was in the kitchen eating an apple. Even though I could probably pack for a vacation in the bags under his eyes, as soon as he saw me, a huge grin spread across his face.

"Morning."

"Morning. Thanks for sleeping in the chair. It had to be uncomfortable."

"Not too bad. How'd you sleep? I heard music on in our room so I figured you went in there and did your geeky music thing."

I playfully punched his arm and he faked injury. "It is not geeky. We just happen to love music."

"Don't get me wrong. I love music too. I just don't need to spend hours on end dissecting the lyrics looking for hidden meaning."

"Fair enough, I guess. Maybe it is pretty geeky, but I love it."

"You both do. So, how are you doing this morning?"

A chill spread through me. "Okay, I guess. Just feel a bit drained. I had this crazy dream. It felt so real." I shivered.

He crossed the kitchen in an instant, and put a hand on my shoulder before pulling me into a hug. "Hey, hey. Don't worry about it. It was just a dream after all." He moved his hands to my face, forcing me to look him in the eyes. "Everything will be alright. Your dad will be home on Sunday, remember?"

I nodded and gave him a quick peck on the cheek, then thanked him and headed for the front door when I heard Lucas calling for me to leave. I grabbed my backpack, opened the door and nearly bumped into someone. My dad's best friend and partner at his doctor's office was standing on the front porch with a man I didn't recognize. A police officer. I instantly felt light headed as every detail of my dream came flooding back.

"Mac?"

"Hey, kiddo. Can I come in?"

Ethan walked out from the kitchen as Lucas pulled me aside, ushering Mac and the officer into the living room.

Ethan was the first to speak. "What's going on?"

"Well, I have something I need to tell Samantha. You boys should probably hear this too, though it's really hard for me. I don't know how to say it."

I couldn't move. I stood at the open door, staring at my dad's best friend and as if on queue, the sky opened up. As rain beat on the windows and silence filled the room, my heart ripped painfully into pieces. My vision blurred and I doubled over, emptying the contents of my stomach onto the floor. In a mess of tears and vomit, my world broke open. I shook, unable to control the rise of despair that filled every inch of me.

"Sam!" Lucas knelt beside me and held my hair.

"Oh, God. Oh, God."

"Sam. Calm down. Everything will be okay."

"Please. Please don't let it be true, Lucas. Please tell me he isn't here to tell me my dream came true."

"Sit over here." He steered me towards the couch. "Let me handle this."

As he crossed the room to talk to Mac, Ethan sat down next to me, wiping my face with a warm, damp cloth. He folded my hand into his and rubbed my back as I continued to sob.

"Sam, honey." Mac knelt in front of me. "I am so sorry. Your father was killed transporting medical supplies between villages. They believe it was a gang of men known to roam the area. They killed everyone in the van. I am so sorry…"

His words disappeared as if someone had hit the mute button. I saw his lips moving, I saw tears well up in his eyes but I heard nothing. I saw him reach out for my hand but I couldn't feel him. There wasn't anything I could say to him. There wasn't anything I could say to anyone. As my world crashed around me the only thing I was conscious of was Ethan holding my hand and I held on to it for dear life.

Chapter 4

April
Pensacola, Florida

"Dad!" I screamed in terror. Tangled up in my sheets and sweaty from my restless memory, I screamed, "Daddy!"

Lucas came running like the world was on fire and was at my side, shaky with concern, before I could bellow another syllable. Instead I just cried giant, breathless tears that had no end. He held me and rocked me until I gained some semblance of composure. Every muscle in my body ached from some otherworldly fight. Still uncertain, I opened my eyes and allowed them to adjust to the quiet darkness. It was then I noticed Ethan on the other side of the bed holding my hand, head bowed and murmuring something I couldn't understand. With every word he uttered, my terror eased and I became, for lack of a better word, hopeful. Calm. As if he could sense my ease, Lucas loosened his grip and began to stroke my hair.

"Are you alright, Sam? We're here. Nothing is going to happen to you. We're here."

We're here. For reasons beyond my understanding those words both comforted and frightened me.

"I had that dream again. It was terrible and beautiful." My voice hitched. "I saw my dad again."

Ethan stopped his whispers for a moment to inquire, "Was it the same as the last time you saw him?"

"Kind of. It was that whole 'my turn' dream again. He was telling me it was my turn now. But there was more to it, this time. There was more clarity. More caution."

The box. The box that had been haunting my dreams since my father died. The box that called out to me. I had no idea what it meant. All I knew was it just showed up one day in my dreams, like an omen. Warning me of my father's death. Warning of some impending doom that I was now supposed to get ready for. It all seemed so real.

I'd done everything I could think of to forget about the damn box but it wouldn't let me. All I wanted to do was a moment to mourn my dad. I wanted to miss him for just a little while without some weird vision interrupting me.

Yet, I knew I needed to see it again. I was sure I was supposed to have it.

"What do you remember? Sam, tell me everything," Lucas said, his voice demanding.

"I'm just repeating myself. Every day you tell me to tell you what I remember. It's the same, just, I don't know, *more*."

Ethan's tone was easy, "I know, Sam. We just have to be sure."

"Be sure of what?"

"We don't know yet."

Everyday for the past two weeks it was the same 'we don't know yet' answer. I just wanted the dream to go away. I knew it meant something. I just didn't know what.

"I remember a package on my doorstep," I began. Somehow, Ethan's touch gave me the courage to allow the words to come out. I took comfort in the feeling that I could somehow tell he was afraid for me.

"It has no return address. My name is written on the paper and the script floats and shimmers. I remember Ethan comes in and scares me. The box is inside the package. Another word, Hope, is written in another language. I cut my hand."

Lucas took a deep breath and asked, "What do you remember about the box?"

"Nothing," I said, shaking my head. "Except you said something about Hope. I don't remember anything other than that. I cut my hand and passed out. Oh, and the lid. It was carved. Beautiful. And familiar somehow."

"Okay. Are you sure it wasn't just the same dream again? You're pretty tired and…"

"Look, there was more." I hated it when Ethan patronized me. "I may be kept under lock and key for the past two weeks but there was more to that dream and I remembered it all. It was terrible and beautiful. Frightening and serene. It made me feel like I was supposed to go to it. To the box. And my dad has something to do with it."

The boys exchanged a glance that I couldn't mistake. They knew I was telling the truth. It was almost as if they expected it.

Without allowing them to interject, I continued. "I am somewhere dark. Dark and mountainous with the sea below me. There is so much sadness. So much anger. In the distance I see swirls of light shooting through the sky. It's like they are locked in some strange dance. One is ominously dark and the other is beautifully golden. I can't stop focusing on them. They seem to move closer every time I blink. I hear this amazing humming sound. It's everywhere. I thought I would go deaf with the noise.

46

Then I see my dad, like I told you before. He says it's *my turn*." I shook my head, anticipating their next question. "No, no. He doesn't explain this time. That part is exactly the same."

"Maybe you *did* have the same dream all over again," Lucas stated softly.

I stood up and eyed them defiantly. I wasn't going to let them brush this off again. I surprised myself, wondering why I would think such a thing. Why *would* they?

With anger in my blood, I continued, "You aren't listening. I said there was more. Not only does the box arrive on my doorstep, but also I touch it, bleed on it. Hope. I remember the word Hope. Then I see my dad and when he leaves, a girl appears. She isn't exactly a girl, considering she has wings. True, they are the most beautiful wings I've ever seen, but for Christ's sake, they are still *wings!* Not wings like a bird, but more like a fairy or a pixie.

"When she speaks, all the buzzing stops. The wind dies down and the sea becomes placid, like a lake. She tells me I have to train. I have to help her. She's sad. She's so sad. But she tells me I can't let anyone make me think my dad was anything other than a good man. That I have to keep his memory. That I would 'teeter on the edge of darkness.' Oh, and she tells me I would be betrayed before I could succeed. Whatever that means."

The room was so quiet I could hear nothing but my ragged breathing. Lucas' eyes were fixed to the floor and Ethan was staring at me like I had just told him I was dying.

"What? What?" My words sounded hysterical even to me. Lucas and Ethan looked at each other for a long moment.

Softly, Ethan broke the silence, "She knows. It's time to tell her everything."

"No," Lucas retorted. "It's still too early. We haven't heard from the others. They're supposed to tell us when it's time. She isn't ready yet."

"Time for what? Ready for what? What're you two talking about?"

Ethan continued, "Lucas, you might be the one in charge, the one they communicate through but I'm protecting her, too. Training her, too. We began her training without their consent, so we can tell her this without it as well."

"Ethan, I don't know. I don't know why we haven't heard from them. I don't know why we've been given no instruction. This is a special case. This has never happened before."

"Then it's up to us. It was up to us to start up her training. Now it's up to us to tell her the truth." Ethan pleaded.

"Stop it! Stop it now!" An uncomfortably familiar anger bubbled out of me and I began to pace. "Don't talk about me like I'm not here! Don't talk about me like I'm some special *job* you've been given. You're talking about taking me from my home." Surprise flashed across their faces but only briefly. "Don't think I can't hear your whispered conversations. You won't let me talk about that god-forsaken box that keeps intruding on my thoughts other than when you think it's necessary. I can't even grieve for my father. This damned dream won't let me. And I miss him!" My eyes welled with tears. "I miss him and I want to be able to miss him without disturbing thoughts, unwelcome visions and voices that fill my head with fear and anxiety."

My voice pitched on the edge of insanity but I didn't care. "Well, it seems my safety, my life, is in danger and you two are bickering over whether or not you should tell me something that's obviously important. Well, screw you. It's my goddamn life, for Christ's sake! So talk! Tell me what is going on. I know something is out there. Something is happening and it feels, well, it feels evil.

"I hear these voices in my head." I brought my hands up to cover my ears. "Always with the voices. They keep telling me to run. I see my dad in my dreams and all he tells me is it's my freakin' turn with no goddamned explanation. Then I see a fairy girl *thing* and I know she's real. It isn't a dream. I *know* she's *real*. And she talks of betrayal and success."

I stopped pacing and stared at them. "I trust you because I somehow know there's something dangerous around me. I feel it in my bones that I'm somehow a part of it. Ever since that stupid box showed up in my head, my thinking has changed. My life has changed and, by God, you're going to tell me or I'm going to walk. I'll walk the hell away and I won't look back. I'll find out, on my own, what's happening to me and what happened to my father. I'll find out who and what you really are." Again, surprise flicked in their eyes as I jabbed a finger at the two of them. "Yeah, that much I figured out. And I don't give a rat's ass about safety or protocol or whatever the hell you two are confused about. You talk or I will make you miserable in a way that I know deep down only I can. Understand?"

Both boys stared at me as if they'd never met me before and I knew I was no closer to an explanation. My generally laid back persona had disappeared as soon as I let the anger and grief take the lead. I felt like I was drowning in shadows. I radiated darkness and shook with frustration. I seethed. Turning on my heel, I stormed out of the room, making sure the door slammed hard enough to let them know I meant it.

I walked outside and no one followed. I shoved my earbuds into my cars and shuffled through the playlists on my iPod. Volume at nearly full blast and the song on repeat, I waited for Fred Durst to start breaking stuff. I smiled wickedly when I realized it was the perfect song for my sour mood.

Running like I was on fire, I darted through the neighborhood to the community park and followed the path for about two miles until I came to the creek. This was my thinking spot. My decompression zone. I started pacing, shaking out the muscles in my arms that had tightened up. I couldn't stop vibrating with anger, fear and whatever else I couldn't describe. It was all a bit too intense and I was having trouble talking myself back down. I could feel myself drowning in it.

At that moment, I just wished for my life to go back to what it was. I wanted to finish high school, go to prom, start college and whatever else I knew would be taken from me. I screamed as loud as I could and plopped down at the edge of the water.

Skipping rocks across the creek, I decided to practice the new little trick I'd discovered. I looked around to see if anyone had followed me but, with a knot in my stomach, I realized no one had. I hurled the first rock as hard and far as I could. It shattered to dust on a tree trunk on the opposite side of the creek. I stared at my hand. *That wasn't part of the trick.*

Tossing the next one, I watched as it bounced across the water and disappeared. I focused on the spot where it sank and concentrated. Shakily, I held out my hand and slowly the rock crept out of the water and skipped back toward me, back into my hand. I practiced my technique for the next half hour, trying to get the rock to move in a fluid motion, and smiling as I thought about the fact that I hadn't told the boys about it.

They've kept secrets from me; I was keeping this from them.

But, it would be kind of cool to show them this. I hadn't practiced on anything bigger than a fist-sized rock and I began to wonder if I could do it on something larger.

Looking around, I saw a small, fallen tree. Dusting myself off and zipping up my hoodie, I walked over to the log and inspected it. The tree's trunk was no thicker than my forearm and had snapped off near the base, leaving a short stump sticking out of the ground. I placed one hand over the rotted stump and another over the fallen tree. In my head I focused on the tree and pictured it whole and undamaged. The air around me began to twirl in anticipation as energy crept back into the tree. With a shudder, the air died down and I opened my eyes. The tree was whole again, its leaves green and lush. *No way. That's seriously cool.*

That little experiment had sapped my energy. *No pun intended*, I chuckled to myself. I found a mossy spot next to the now healed tree and sat down. I stared at the lush leaves and I plucked one off to examine it. *How did I do that?* I shook my head in disbelief yet unable to stop myself from smiling at the same time. I had no idea what was going on and I wished I knew. I sat there for a long time, snapping twigs and putting them back together. Finally, allowing Sarah McLachlan to calm me, I closed my eyes.

I knew there was something different about me. I felt stronger. I felt faster. And, oh yeah, I could fix broken trees and recall sunken pebbles from underwater. *Weird.*

An ever-closer danger that I needed to face filled the silence. I knew Lucas wasn't what he appeared to be. I'd known him my whole life. He was my best friend but I couldn't help but feel he was becoming something more, something different. And the farther away we got from the day I first dreamt of the box, I couldn't help but feel that Ethan had changed, too.

Once carefree and fun Lucas had slowly morphed into a responsible leader in constant sync with some set of rules that I didn't quite understand but never questioned. He was quick to demand knowledge of my whereabouts, like I was going anywhere, anyway. Planning and discussion had replaced his usually spontaneous personality.

There were other times I caught myself daydreaming about Ethan, who had never shown concrete romantic interest in me. But, for some reason, I felt like there was something between us that, if explored, would be combustible. Almost as if it would be the most amazing experience ever, if it worked out. And if it didn't, it would be more explosive than a nuke. The butterflies I felt for Lucas all growing up settled over the years into something more comfortable. I like it. With Ethan, it wasn't so much butterflies as it was a category four churning in my belly.

All the secrecy and whispers was irritating. I didn't quite know what was in store for me, as I had yet to be privy to the information. And anger at my ignorance overcame any immediate trust I once felt.

Sure, I knew Ethan and Lucas only had my best interest at heart but it was high time I stepped up and took some control back.

Samantha, run! Now!

Yanking my earbuds out of my ears, I whipped my head around. While throwing myself an amazing pity party, an unnatural darkness had rolled in. I hadn't heard the hum begin or felt the wind pick up. My self-absorption was all consuming, at least until I'd heard that one word. I tried to peer into the growing darkness.

Not now. Adrenaline pumped through my veins. My surroundings swam and my vision lost focus.

Run!

My legs wouldn't allow me to run and all I could do was stand and brace myself for whatever was coming. I needed to get the hell out of there but for some reason, I couldn't. The strange darkness slunk through the trees and pulsed menacingly. Wind screamed at me, fierce and angry, sending leaves scurrying and bending whole trees as they keeled over in defense. I should've been frightened out of my skin, but I was only half so. I was in awe.

Focus slowly returned when I heard footsteps running toward me. "Sam! Sam! Where are you?"

"Here, Ethan! I'm here. Something's happening."

Ethan came bursting out of the trees, his hand reaching for me. "I know. I know. We have to get back to the house! Let's go!"

I stood my ground in spite of what was happening around me. My previous anger at the two of them returned with a vengeance. The darkness enveloped us as the hum took over. And, suddenly, the earth groaned as towering trees ripped out of the ground and slammed down around us, roots flailing helplessly in the wind.

Still, I stood defiant. "No. I won't come with you unless you promise to tell me what's happening! Ethan, I know something's going on. Just look around us, for Christ's sake! I need to know!"

Run!

The wind howled, as darkness drew ever closer, not even a sliver of early morning light remained. The clouds thickened and I swore my hearing had gotten ten times better despite the deafening hum. There was no shrinking away from the fear that was coming. I could feel it. It was the kind of fear that would consume me, destroy me. I embraced it and at the same time I was utterly repulsed by it.

Now, Samantha. Run!

My head turned in every direction as I searched for the source of the voice. Dad? Was that my dad telling me to run?

Ethan pleaded, "I will, I swear. You just have to come with me now. It isn't safe here. I know you think you're ready. I know we haven't been fair by keeping the truth from you. But we'll tell you, I swear to God. You just have to take my hand now and you have to come with me. Now, Sam."

His shouts were drowned out under the low reverberations that shuddered through the woods. I followed his lead and we ran back toward the house. Something was following us. Something was trying to get inside me, like it was trying to rip me open. The noise was terrible. Trees continued to explode from the earth all around us. I was just about to turn around when I heard my dad's voice again.

I am here, Samantha. Listen to Ethan. I'll do what I can from here.

I stopped running and yelled into the wind, "Dad! Where are you?"

Just go. I will keep you safe.

The sky lit up for a split second and an enormous boom of thunder followed almost immediately. I could see the wind whipping around us but, for some reason, it didn't touch us as we ran. Silence surrounded us like a bubble though I knew beyond our cocoon the noise was deafening. I sprinted faster than I'd ever had. Logs and trees fell to block my path and I hurdled them easily. Enormous sinkholes appeared as the ground opened up, trying to swallow me, but I flew over them. Trees and branches reached out to snare me, tearing at my skin and shredding my clothes, trying to slow me down.

As we burst out of the park into the neighborhood, I slowed for a minute. None of the other houses were subjected to the assault. I stopped running and stood inform of an old colonial just a block down from my own home. There was no sign the damaging winds were affecting it.

"Sam! Duck!"

Ethan grabbed me and we hit the sidewalk as a tree branch slipped through the protective bubble that surrounded us.

"What the hell?"

"Not now, Sam. Move. Get back to the house."

As we ran, Ethan tripped and fell. "Just go Samantha!"

I bounded up the porch steps and saw Lucas, hands outstretched, yelling into the fury. Ethan was rushing to join us. Behind him, a whirl of darkness and a glow of light tangled together like a pair of cyclones. Trees uprooted and crashed into each other in mid-air. Ethan made it onto the porch just as a flash of light dropped us to the ground and our three bodies slammed against the front door. The darkness became still and silent. Ethan shielded me with his body while Lucas shielded Ethan with his. A massive tree hit the ground right in front of the house and probably should've crushed us had it been any closer. We were covered in leaves and grass but, other than a few bumps and bruises, were almost entirely unscathed. Another crack of thunder scrambled me to my feet. Silent darkness descended around us.

We tore into the house and slammed the door shut. Out of breath, we slowly sank to the floor, our backs against the steel paneled entrance. For a few minutes we just sat there, huddled together, trying to ward off a chill that had seeped into our bones.

Chapter 5

Antsy, I untangled myself from our huddle and shakily walked into the kitchen. My throat felt like a dry and the cold water I gulped down did nothing to moisten it. Standing at the sink, I peered through the window into the darkness that had refused to recede. It looked like a tornado had blown my yard and had missed the rest of the houses in the neighborhood. The only outside proof was a dark cloudy sky. Examining myself for injuries, I was amazed to find I had none. Trees were fallen everywhere. I could feel a barrier protecting us just as I could feel that whatever else was out there was stalking us, lying in wait. Waiting to pounce.

Though a light rain had begun to fall, the sun was trying it's best to break through the clouds. I knew it was my dad out there. My dad who kept me safe. Yet I also knew it was impossible. *He's dead, Sam.*

"Sam," Ethan began. "Are you okay?"

My eyes remained fixated on the destruction outside and I answered in a barely audible whisper. "Yeah. Are you?"

With a smirk, Ethan tried to lighten the mood, "Yeah. You know me, Sam. Indestructible."

"I really don't think any of this is funny, Ethan."

"I know, Sam. I know." Ethan sighed. "I've been rehearsing this conversation and I still can't get it right."

Whirling around to face him, my words came out poisonous. "Why don't you start by answering a few questions? What was that, Ethan?" I yelled, pointing at the window. "What was happening out there? I was afraid but I felt that I was supposed to fight whatever was coming. And when we ran back to the house, I out ran you. For the first time, *you, Ace,* couldn't keep up with *me*. What the hell's happening? What was that God awful noise and why the hell is my father, who is dead, by the way, telling me to run?"

Lucas came into the kitchen, his voice rough, "Calm down."

"Screw you, Lucas! What was that?"

"You really need to calm down. Now." Lucas reached out and grabbed my arm as he spoke. His face twisted for just a moment into something I didn't recognize. A weird dark energy suddenly surged around him, then dissipated just as quickly. It was as if I'd never seen him before.

Ethan interrupted, his voice calm. "I think you need to sit down, Samantha. We have a lot to talk about, a lot to explain. It's time we told you. They found you and we can no longer protect you without divulging everything. And we don't have much time left. You need to be ready and we haven't been doing the best job at preparing you." For an instant, before determination set itself in Ethan's eyes, they softened as he looked at me.

"Who found me? The people that killed my dad?"

"You need to listen. Ask as many questions as you want but right now, you need to listen."

My head high, I avoided contact with either of them as we walked to the kitchen table and sat down. I had no idea what they were going to tell me but I knew in my bones that it was going to change everything. A rise of jumbled emotions settled itself somewhere behind my rationality and I had to concentrate to tame it. Lucas took hold of my hand, for my comfort or his, I couldn't really say. Either way, I pulled my hand away and placed it in my lap, my eyes daring them to try and weasel out this yet again.

Ethan played with his bottom lip as he tried to figure out how to begin. *Odd*. Lately, he'd been so confident but I saw confusion setting into him now.

"It's okay, Ethan. I'm ready for whatever you have to tell me. And, after what I just saw outside, I don't think much could shock me at this point."

The look on his face filled me with the notion that I might be wrong and apprehension knotted in my belly. We all sat in silence for what seemed like hours though I knew the clock had only ticked away a few minutes. Lucas was alternating between bouncing his knees and drumming his fingers on the table, both of which were annoying. I quickly put my hand over his to quiet him. Ethan rubbed his hands over his eyes to ward off exhaustion. I was growing impatient, waiting for him to begin but he spoke before I could prompt him further.

"Sam, before we begin, I want to ask you a couple of questions. We might be able to explain some of the things you've been experiencing. Answer some of the questions you may have. But it's important that we know exactly what you know and what you don't. It will help us determine the right course of action. Only then will we be able to understand what happened today."

I nodded and Ethan took a large breath that filled his cheeks. Blowing it out slowly, he looked at me, his eyes intense. I met his stare with one of incredulity. Funny that I already didn't believe him, even before he opened his mouth.

"What do you remember about your father?"

"What do I remember? You're talking like he's been gone for years. His funeral was just a few weeks ago, remember?"

"Please, Sam. Just answer the question."

Surprise tingled my skin as my defiance continued to rise and there was nothing I could do to control it. "My father?" I knew the tone of my response was uncalled for. The shrill pitch alone had me cringing inwardly. I just couldn't control any of it. Anger, rage, fury, and defiance – they were all minions, clearing the path for the darkness to set in.

Lucas answered softly, trying to defuse the irrational emotions pouring out of me. "Quite a bit, actually. But we need to know what you remember. It will be easier to fill in the blanks that way. It's important that you leave no detail out. You tell us all you remember and we will tell you all we know."

Fair deal, I supposed.

"Well," I stammered and bit my lip. "Jeez, I mean, he was my dad. You knew him. He was the funniest person I knew. Right? No matter how bad of a day I had, he could always make me feel better. He was the best."

They both watched me in silence, waiting for me to continue.

"He was a doctor, so he worked a lot, especially toward the end, always traveling out of the country to do charity work. He was shot by a group of men that were hijacking his van. They never caught the guys who did it. He loved his job but his job got him killed." I still hadn't had the chance to grieve the loss of my dad and here they were, making me relive that morning all over again. Anger bubbled through me and I clenched my hands to keep from slamming them against the table. "You guys know all this. Why do I have to explain all of this to you now? You've both known him forever. You've practically lived with us since Jack died. Sometimes I think you two knew him better than I did. It's frustrating."

The glance they shared pissed me off even more. The whole "dun, dun, dunnn... let's look at each other for suspense" thing was becoming really old. But my annoyance was the only thing that kept me from falling to pieces.

"Okay, only some of what you just said is true, Sam," Ethan told me. "He wasn't really a doctor. And though he was killed by a man, we know exactly who killed him. And because we know that, you're right when you say we knew him better."

"I'm sorry, what? Wait. Wait. Wait." I threw my hands up in disbelief. "He was too a doctor. He worked at the hospital until he joined the Doctors

Without Borders program. He shared his practice with Mac." I stopped. "Wait, I don't understand. You say you know who killed him? Have you told the police?"

"No, Sam. In this life he was a doctor. In his real life he wasn't so much a doctor as a…a healer. And we can't tell the police. Even if they believed us, which I doubt, they'd never be able to catch who did it."

I saw nothing but shadows as my world started to buzz. Faint whispers stung my ears but I couldn't make out what was being said. All I could think about was that Lucas and Ethan were lying to me. I trusted them and they were lying to me. How could I believe any of this? I didn't even know which part of the lie to focus on first.

"If you know who did it then call the FBI. Call *someone*. Someone must know what to do!"

"We can't, Sam," Ethan said.

"Like hell you can't."

"It isn't possible," Lucas interjected. "No one would take us seriously if we were to tell them the truth."

I gave Lucas a look that should've killed him instantly. I was overflowing with anger. "How do you know? You haven't told the authorities? My dad was murdered and you sit here doing nothing? Truth?" I slammed my hands onto the table. "You have no idea what the word means."

Ethan stepped in before icicles could shoot from my eyes and kill his brother. "We can't because he wasn't human."

I was momentarily paralyzed by this absurd revelation.

The familiar sensation of weight falling off my shoulders eased through me and I felt suddenly light, like I'd finally been freed from a straight jacket. I'd slipped outside of myself again. It had been happening ever since I could remember. Sometimes I was amused when it happened. It was kind of funny to watch myself when I had no control over what my body was doing. Other times, like now, all I wanted was to regain control quickly so I could try to reason through what was being said.

Right then, in that state, I was merely a puppet. A slave to whichever emotion decided to take over. And each time it happened, everything got a little darker, a little more muted. Colors washed each other out like a Monet painting was being rinsed off its canvas. Until my emotions calmed, all I could do was helplessly watch the interaction and hope I didn't do anything regrettable.

I could see my body still seated at the table across from Ethan and Lucas. The look on my face was absolutely priceless. "Who wasn't human?" I was saying. "My dad? The people who killed him? You really need to clarify what the hell you two are talking about."

"Both," Lucas offered, clearly having no idea there were now two of me in the room.

"Both what?"

"Both. Your dad and the one who killed him."

I watched myself stand up and stare Lucas in the eye. He shivered as if he could feel ice roll off me. "Wait just a damn minute. You're telling me that my dad wasn't human? He was killed by 'people' who aren't human? What the hell have you two been smoking? You're forgetting just one little thing here: he's as real as you and me. And if he wasn't, what does that make me? A freakin' alien?"

"No, Sam," Ethan said. "Your dad was an angel. His job was to protect others. He was kind of like a doctor but a little more…" Struggling to find the word, Ethan looked at Lucas. For a few seconds neither of them spoke. Neither could seem to find the right word to explain it.

I could see my head whip as I looked back and forth between them. I had never been more confused and it didn't look like I'd be educated on what was happening anytime soon. I could feel my body roiling in defiance.

69

"A little more ethereal," Lucas finally said.

My other self stopped and stared at the two incredulously as some immoveable anger rattled inside my body. "Shut up. What're you talking about? Do you even hear yourselves? You both must've taken crazy pills this morning. I won't sit here and listen to this half-assed explanation. Somebody better start telling me the truth or I swear to God…"

"Don't do that," Lucas growled fiercely.

"Don't do what?" My other self snapped back.

"Don't swear to God."

"Lucas, really?" That was it. I could feel the last thread of my rationality quickly unraveling. "Screw you! And screw God! He took my dad, so excuse me if my manners aren't up to par in order to satisfy some random deity that, as of a month ago, doesn't exist to me. Angels? You've got to be fucking kidding me. Screw you. Screw both of you."

Ethan stepped between us, trying to referee. "Sam, we know it's hard to believe. We know it's a lot to take in, but you have to let us explain."

"Explain? You want me to let you *explain*?" I could see and feel my body begin to shake uncontrollably. "You know what? The only thing I want you to do is shut up. Just shut up! Just stop." My other self shoved her hand at Ethan's face. "This isn't funny. My dad was a doctor. A doctor! He woke up every morning and ate his Cheerios with a glass of OJ and a cup of coffee, heavy on the sugar and cream. He got dressed, every day, in his shirt and tie, his stethoscope and spit shined shoes. He would come home, exhausted. He would take a shower like a normal human being after a hard day of work. We took turns making dinner. We watched baseball together and swam in our pool. He took his boat out on the weekends. He loved to fish." I could feel tears sting my eyes.

"Damn it! He broke his thumb building me a swing set when I was seven! What kind of angel breaks their thumb? Just shut up! Don't tell me I don't know my dad. He was all I had. He tucked me in every damn night, Ethan. Don't you fucking tell me about *my* dad. He was real. He hugged me and kissed me and loved me. And now he's dead. How can a fucking angel die?"

Horrified and helpless, I watched myself try to furiously storm out of the kitchen but Lucas suddenly blocked my path. Jesus, how'd he move so fast? Wasn't he just sitting down?

"Sam…"

I saw the dark glint in my eye. Words, both deliberate and out of character, escaped my lips. "Get out of my way, Lucas, or I swear - *to God* – I. Will. Hurt. You." As I watched the words leave my lips and hang above my body like some stupid cartoon bubble, the room became hazy. The kitchen window imploded, shattering glass shards all over Lucas.

Ethan covered his head in defense then rushed around the table, and grabbing my shoulders, whispered my name. He shook me but I couldn't respond. I was no longer observing, but I was at a complete loss for words. Everything inside me froze solid with trepidation. I had no idea what just happened. I had no idea why it had happened. What the hell did I just do? Unsure of myself, I met Ethan's gaze. He was searching my eyes for something that he couldn't find. I took a step back to survey the kitchen. Glass was everywhere. The frame of the window was still intact but all the glass had shattered.

Ethan moved to help Lucas but he stopped him. "No, Ethan. Let her do it."

"What?" Ethan looked more confused than when the window had shattered. At least someone was feeling the way I was.

"It's okay, Ethan. Sam can fix it. Can't you, Sam?"

My eyes finally focused on Lucas. He was covered in glass, bleeding everywhere and I slowly realized that he knew. I didn't know how but he knew my secret. But he knew I could fix broken things. Shame washed over me at the fact that I'd kept this from them and Lucas had known all along. Who was I kidding? I wasn't surprised, not really. They knew everything, anyway. They always knew everything. For the past few years, our minds had been so in sync that we'd been able to finish each other's sentences.

"I don't understand. Are you saying…?" Ethan looked from me to Lucas.

"Sam is a healer, Ethan. Like James. I've seen her practicing in the woods. It's amazing, really. I almost didn't believe it myself. She can do this. She can heal me. Go on, Sam. Fix it. Focus. Concentrate, just like you do in the woods. Just like the twigs and branches and trees earlier today. Make the window whole again. I know you can do it. I've seen you do it. I have faith in you. I trust you. Show Ethan what I'm talking about."

Unsure, I slowly stepped over the broken glass, past Lucas. Ethan stared at me like he'd caught me in a lie and I quickly looked away from him. I was going to need to concentrate and I couldn't do it while looking at him. I positioned myself between the window and Lucas. Glass glittered all around him and I could see trickles of blood on his arms and face where some of the shards had buried themselves.

Extending one hand to the window and the other to Lucas, I closed my eyes and concentrated. I focused on making the window solid again. I envisioned pulling those shards from Lucas's skin. The air started swimming as the energy heated up. My concentration faltered a bit when I began to think about healing Lucas. A twig, a branch, even a tree – so not the same as a person. Recalling rocks from water was not willing glass to exit a body. I shook my head and forced myself to focus.

You can do this, Samantha. Focus.

Dad? Could it really be him? All I wanted to do was curl up into a ball and cry but I knew feeling sorry for myself wouldn't help anyone. I summoned every bit of energy I had and concentrated on what I had to do. In my mind I saw myself healing Lucas. I saw him unmarred.

When I opened my eyes, I looked up at Lucas. He was giving me the most brilliant smile I'd ever seen and I was all the more determined to make amends. Palms fixed on my targets, I used all my energy to concentrate on the task at hand. The air whirled around me like a mini indoor tornado and everything began to tingle as the atmosphere became electric. My lips began to move and voice unfamiliar words. Just as quickly all was still and silent.

I looked at the window. Not a crack. I walked over and placed my palm on the pane that was still warm to the touch but otherwise in one piece. I looked over at Lucas. Not a scratch. I slowly made my way over to him and began to trace my fingers where I knew there was glass a minute before. I followed where the blood had run. Nothing. My heart jumped. I'd healed him. With a shaky smile, I slowly pulled my hand away.

Holy hell.

My legs became jelly and I dropped to the floor. My head was pounding. I stared at my palms as I suddenly became very hot. It felt like it was over a hundred degrees in the kitchen and sweat pooled at my brow. I felt faint. My vision swam a bit and I knew I needed to calm down, relax. My stomach flip-flopped and it felt like a million bugs were crawling all over me but I was too weak to brush them off. Ethan sat cross-legged directly in front of me. Taking my hands in his, he told me to close my eyes and when I did, I saw light and darkness intertwine. I saw the shadows inside me dissipate though I somehow knew they would return. I felt the cool touch of softness surround me. My legs were no longer rubber and my headache had eased.

Ethan let go of my hands and smiled wryly. He brushed the hair out of my eyes. I had to look away before he saw my embarrassment. Before he saw through me. Looking more proud than angry, he said, "Well, well, well. Our little Sammy's been holding out on us."

Blushing from confusion, I said, "Yeah, I guess."

Still smiling, Ethan said, "It's okay. I'm impressed. It's satisfying to know some of your gifts have started to shine through. You're definitely a healer. Like your dad, like me. Now we know where to focus our training. We've been doing this blind so far. I know you probably need to rest but it's very important we get through this conversation sooner rather than later."

I took his hand as he pulled me to my feet, "I'm okay. I need to continue or I think I might just punk out."

"You're braver than that, Sam. We know you are. And even if we didn't, that little display would've proved otherwise."

Again with the confusing statements. I wondered when I was going to understand. Sighing, I faced Lucas. He was smiling though I knew he should've been angry with me.

"Lucas, I'm really sorry. I never meant to…"

"It's fine, Sam. I promise. But before we start over, I think you need to see something. This isn't easy for me to show you but I feel, in order to speed this process along, you need to see it."

A sudden burst of light momentarily blinded me. For a second I felt like a cornered dog that needed to strike out, a little disoriented and a lot defensive. I turned my head towards Lucas. It was a moment before I realized he was shirtless. Mesmerized by his amazing abs, I struggled to return his gaze.

What the…

He was almost glowing as a faint trace of light outlined his body and the most beautiful and vibrant colors I'd ever seen surrounded him. His eyes had taken on the vividness of a fresh rainbow. Slowly, the gleaming hues expanded like an unfurling flag. It was as if the whole kitchen had been taken over by a box of crayons. Wild and surreal shades of gold, amber, and red blended softly as they stretched out beside him. All at once, in unison, massive appendages pulsed back and forth. Light ebbed and flowed with the movement. His posture tightened and his hands reached out to his sides. It was the most beautiful and captivating image I'd ever seen. My hand flew to my mouth as I took it in.

Lucas had wings.

"Oh, my God. Lucas…" I was mesmerized and astonished at what was spread out before me.

For a moment he looked embarrassed, "I wanted to tell you, Samantha. It's been so hard keeping this side of myself from you."

"I've known you my whole life and all along you've been a, uh…"

"An angel," Ethan stepped in.

Whirling around to look at him, I almost forgot he was there. "An angel? Like, uh, a real live angel? As in, from heaven?" God, I knew he was amazing but this was unreal.

"Ha-ha. Kind of. I was born an angel but I only got my wings a couple years ago."

"A couple years ago? But isn't that when…"

"My dad died. Yes." He struggled for the words. "I inherited this gift when he died."

"So, your dad was an angel? He looked like you? Why doesn't Ethan have wings?" I turned to face Ethan. "Are you an angel too?" As I said this, I turned Ethan around and inspected his back like I was expecting to suddenly see something sprout from his shoulder blades.

"Yes. I don't have my wings, though." He looked embarrassed. "It's a huge misconception thinking all angels have wings. Some of us have them when we are born, some don't. Some get them later in life. I may get them soon; I may have to wait awhile. We honestly don't know why that is. We do know, however, that we've all been put here for a purpose. That purpose is to protect those who aren't like us. We were put in place after our father died to protect you. You were a special case though. A special case considering who your father was. He was stronger than most."

"Who my father was? You said he was an angel, too."

"He was. He was a powerful angel. He was a healer. He was able to protect those around him through special incantations and prayers. His work took him to some dangerous places. That's why we were called upon to protect you when he couldn't be near. We weren't needed, really. His protection reached you no matter where he was."

"But he died."

"He did. Unlike many of the myths about us, angels can die. We are born as human as we can be, we live among humans, we feel emotion stronger than humans and we can die. It's a bit harder to kill us but it can be done."

As he spoke, Lucas came over and placed my hand on his chest. I could feel his heart beat in rhythm with his wings. I could see the rise and fall of his breathing. He looked, despite the wings, human. With a flash, I remembered the glass, the blood trickling down his arms and face.

Feeling awkward and embarrassed, the words just tumbled out. "I'm so sorry. I didn't know the window would break. That part never happened before. I usually break twigs and branches on purpose so I can fix them."

"No worries. You're just realizing what you can do. Your emotions are quick and unpredictable. You need more practice before you can fully control it. Now I know never to piss you off," Lucas laughed.

I smiled back, "Well, I'm sorry anyway."

It was all still confusing, but made a weird kind of sense at the same time and I was beginning to believe them. I turned to Ethan and said, "So, my dad was an angel. Tell me more about him."

"Your father, like all angels, was a protector first and foremost. His main duty was to protect the Box of Hope. Once you were born, he was bound to keep you safe as well."

"What's the Box of Hope?"

"I think you know, Samantha."

Realization dawned on me. "The box that I see in my dreams. The box with my name on it. But, I don't understand. That's just a dream, right? I mean, it feels real, but how could it be?"

Ethan sat down. "The box is real, Samantha. The location of the box, however, has always been a secret. Your father's secret and the secret of the one before him. There are those who want to see it destroyed and those who want to use it to take over the world. If that box ever got into their hands, they would be more than happy to eliminate all traces of hope in the world. They would rule with fear and submission rather than free will." He paused for a moment, as though choosing his words carefully. "They, apparently, found the location of the box but James got to it before they did. Unfortunately, they found him and killed him. Now we don't know where the box is and we need to find it."

I stared at nothing as I listened to him speak. With each new bit of information I absorbed, I mindlessly wound a string around my finger, tighter and tighter, until the appendage turned white and bloodless.

"That's how we knew he'd died. When you dreamed about it. When you dreamed that you'd opened the package and we saw what lay inside, we knew he was gone. Unfortunately, he died before he could confide any of this to you. He was preparing to tell you about your destiny and help you prefect your gifts. After he died, we took on that responsibility." His smile helped to soften the blow, but only a little. "We knew you'd be special. We weren't sure exactly what your gifts would be, but we were assured, however, that your destiny would be great and we were to prepare to give our lives to keep you safe. We're only two of many, Sam. There's an army of us ready to protect you and what you can bring us."

"Me? You've been trained to die for me? Why? I don't understand." I flopped into the chair across from him, afraid my legs would give out again. "What's so special about me? What could I possibly bring you?"

"You, Samantha, are our hope. The one thing that gives all humans dreams and possibilities. Without it there would be no love, no faith, no joy. The spirit of this hope was placed in a box full of darkness to maintain balance. Because there can't be light without dark, joy without sadness, or love without hate. The box was supposed to remain closed to protect that balance, but the darkness was unleashed when curiosity opened it."

"Curiosity? Like Pandora? But isn't that just a myth?" My mind raced to remember what I'd learned about mythology in history class.

"It isn't entirely a myth. Actually, of all the stories passed down about Pandora and the box, Nathaniel Hawthorne hit the nail on the head. His story, "Pandora and the Great Box", most closely tells the actual story. Of course there are some embellishments but, for the most part, it's entirely accurate."

Ethan pulled a piece of paper from his pocket and unfolded it. It looked as though it had been read many times. I recognized the flowing script that littered the page. It was the same as in my dream. "Nathaniel Hawthorne tells the story of a little girl, Pandora, and her friend Epimetheus. It was Epimetheus who was given the box by a stranger. And, as the story goes, Pandora was so enamored by the beauty of the box and driven by sheer curiosity, she eventually convinced Epimetheus to open it."

"But if they were told not to open it, why would they? Why would this Epi…Epimeep…"

"Epimetheus," Lucas corrected.

"Right. What you said. Why would he open it f he knew he shouldn't?"

"Nothing more than curiosity, it seems. Now in this box, Hope was placed with 'troubles' – all the evils and sins and bad things. And when they opened it, all those troubles escaped and populated society."

"So by opening the box, they allowed despair and hate and all that to thrive? What about hope?"

"Hope was released too. Hope was the only thing keeping those troubles from overtaking everything."

"So this box, left by a stranger, was the Box of Hope?"

"It's just a myth, but the idea is the same."

Chewing my lip, I said, "In my dream, the package was just left at the door for me. There was no one there, no stranger. It seemed as though it had just appeared by itself. The doorbell rings and when I open the door, there's nothing there. Except that wrapped package. But every time I open the package and try to touch the box inside, I wake up without looking inside."

"Right. That much we know," Lucas said. His wings were gone and he'd put his shirt back on. "We can only assume," he explained, "that it was James who sent the box to you. Sort of. He wasn't able to send it to you physically so he reached you in your dreams. Like you, he had the power to heal as well as the power to recall items, like those rocks in the creek. He could also send things away, relocate them, if you will. But was he able to send the box away, to protect it? If so, where? If not, did Sebastian or one of the other Exiled finally get their hands on it? We aren't exactly sure. But we do know James wants you to find it and we have to help you search."

Sitting next to me, he continued. "In addition to his other gifts, and more importantly, your father had the power to destroy darkness. That is what we must find out about you, Sam. We need to know if you can do that as well. If you can do that, and we can find the box, we may be able to finally erase Sebastian and his followers."

"Lucas is right," Ethan said. "In order to fight those who want to take the box, we need to know the full extent of your gifts."

My eyes widened at his words. "Gifts? As in plural?"

Ethan smiled. "Yes, Sam. Plural."

"But where do these gifts come from?"

Lucas walked to the fridge to get me a bottle of water as Ethan stood and began to pace. Confusion swirled around my head and I still couldn't quite wrap my head around any of it.

"All of the angels on earth are descendants of angels that have fallen," Lucas explained. "Some of us have learned the error of the ways of our ancestors and have remained Faithful while others have turned their backs completely on anything good and right. They are called the Exiled, or Dark Angels. They have no hope of gaining favor in their attempts to destroy humankind. They want to rule over humans. They used the gift of free will to fall from heaven and now they want to take it away from all those they deem unworthy, namely humans. Their greed, lust for power and selfishness have made them difficult to destroy. They use promises of riches and fame to pull humans in, often using them as surrogates to produce more Dark Angels."

I shuddered at the thought and looked at Lucas. "And why, exactly, do they want me? Was that them in the woods earlier?"

"Well," Lucas hesitated, trying to find the words. "You're a special case. Like Ethan said, you're the hope we've been looking for. If they can destroy you, or worse yet, convert you to darkness before we find and retrieve the box, there'll be no way for us to fight them."

He sat down at the table beside me and handed me the bottle of water. "We've been fighting a losing battle for centuries," he said. "Generations upon generation of Faithful have either succumbed to the ease with which the Dark Angels live or have died in the pursuit of their destruction. It isn't easy following the Light and remaining faithful to something that seems to have turned Its back on us. We are, after all, fallen as well. It's the only thing we have in common with the others. We tend to get the rough end of the deal as we are unencumbered by greed and fame."

I mulled this over a minute before I spoke. "Well, I can understand how it would be easier to live a life with no financial or material need." I sighed. " So, what you're saying is the Exiled need me to defeat the Faithful and the Faithful need me to defeat the Exiled?"

"In a nutshell, yes," Ethan chimed in.

"Well, I guess it's nice to be wanted," I said through a forced chuckle. "But I'm still confused. Other than his duty to protect the box, how else was my father involved in this battle between the Faithful and the Exiled?"

Ethan was still pacing the kitchen, his nervous energy permeating the room. "James was a very powerful angel. He turned from the darkness when he was a boy. When he saw it destroy his own father."

"My father was a Dark Angel? An Exiled?" If he didn't have my attention before, he had it now. I sat with unwavering focus at his every word.

Ethan seemed in pain as he continued. "He was. But he switched his allegiance. You see, he'd witnessed the destruction caused by following the Exiled and he became unsure of his role. He confided his uncertainty to no one but spent his time learning about the light and the good it brings. He was sick of the lies and chaos brought to all by the Exiled. The last straw was when he saw his own father murdered in front of him."

He stopped in front of the window, his gaze unfocused.

"Your grandfather, Zachary, worked for the most powerful of all Dark Angels, Sebastian. Sebastian had given your grandfather a job. That job was to find and destroy both the Box of Hope and the Heart of Hope. The same box that is now our mission to retrieve. We have no idea where the Heart is, or was, but we do know your father had possession of the box before he died.

"The story goes that your grandfather found the box but, like James, was having doubts as to the intentions of the Exiled. He hid the box away for a time, pretending not to know its location. When Sebastian found out that Zachary had it, he became furious. He paid Zachary a visit one stormy evening, demanding that he hand over the box. Zachary refused. He knew he would be killed for his treason, so he threw a protection spell on your father and tried to send him away. But Sebastian stopped him.

"Knowing the protection spell would keep him from harming your father until he turned eighteen, Sebastian forced James to watch as he murdered his father. Sebastian takes sick pleasure in the pain of others so when he couldn't harm your father physically, he decided to hurt him emotionally."

My eyes welled up at the thought of my father having to watch something so heinous.

"First, Sebastian used the Sword of Death to cut off Zachary's wings, making him become as close to mortal as an angel can be. Though shivering in the most heinous pain one could endure, Zachary refused to bow down in defeat, so Sebastian took the sword and pierced him slowly through the heart, finally killing him."

A shiver ran through me. The shock of how callously my grandfather had been murdered gave me goosc bumps and I had to swallow my nausea.

"Considering Zachary was a Dark Angel, Sebastian was surprised to find light envelope Zachary's body upon his death. Your grandfather had made the leap to the other side without Sebastian knowing. This knowledge angered Sebastian even further and he vowed then and there that he would destroy James and his family. And your dad vowed that he would never again follow darkness and would do whatever was in his power to hide the box from Sebastian and his followers. James spent his life to this pursuit, dodging Sebastian and the others. When he met your mother, he finally experienced the love the Light speaks of and that the Darkness sets out to destroy. He knew, one day, the angel that would restore balance to the fallen angels would return and save us all."

It took a few minutes of breathless shock before I could process all of what Ethan had said. It sounded like a story straight out of some "repent or else" bible study class. I suddenly felt tainted by the knowledge that my family had taken part in the evil of the Exiled, yet proud that they were able to stand up to Sebastian. Could I be that strong? Could I choose right over wrong so easily? Unsure of the answer, I focused on the one thing Ethan said that I did understand.

My mother.

"I never met my mother. My father hardly spoke of her though I know he carried pictures of her in his wallet. There was a chest in the attic that contained some of her things. Clothes, letters, books and some of her jewelry. He wanted everything to stay locked away in the chest. Everything but the one thing he gave me when I turned 16. He told me I would know when to…As a matter of fact…"

I tore out of the kitchen, leaving the boys to gape after me. I took the stairs two at a time up to my room, threw open my closet doors and began to empty hangers. *Not there. Where?* I searched my bag frantically as I tried to find it. Where was it? Cursing myself for my lack of organizational skills, I moved to the top shelf. I wished I had a flashlight. Tumbling stacks of sweaters to the ground, I finally found it. Hidden behind the stack of clothes was the velvet pouch. I peeked inside to make sure what I was looking for was still there and ran back down the steps to the kitchen.

Lucas, looking confused, asked, "What was that all about?"

Feeling a little sentimental but knowing it may have meaning I thrust the bag at him. "My father gave me this. On my sixteenth birthday. He said it was my mother's. He would never let me wear it, though. He told me I wasn't ready but insisted I'd know when I was. Whatever that means."

Gently, Lucas pulled on the golden strings of the emerald pouch to open it. Upending it, the contents spilled into his palm and his eyes widened. He held up a thin, heart shaped pendant made of pure white opal attached to a dainty silver chain. Ethan walked over to Lucas and they both stared at the pendant and then at me, with jaws dropped.

"Pretty, isn't it? A little dull, like it needs to be shined or cleaned. I've never put it on. I was hoping my father would let me know when I could wear it. I've been hiding it in my closet since he gave it to me, though every now and then I would secretly take it out and admire it. I never dared wear it. For some reason, I thought my father would know if I did. I like the way it looks, like it will lay nicely against my skin. Almost as if it's part of me."

Ethan took the necklace and held it to the light. "Sam, do you know what this is?"

"Uh, a necklace?" As I said it, I knew that wasn't the answer they were looking for.

"It's the Heart of Hope," Ethan said. "The Heart of Hope is cut from a single white opal. This is the key to defeating the Exiled."

"I thought the box was the key?"

"It is. The two need to be used together. We have, at least, half of what we need."

I held up my hand. "Wait, I don't understand."

Lucas explained, "As long as the two, the box and the pendant, are separated, both light and dark, hope and despair, continue to thrive. If the two are destroyed, then hope is lost. If, however, the pendant is placed inside the box, much like hope was placed inside Pandora's Box, then despair and all its baggage are extinguished."

"Then why didn't my *father* take my *mother's* pendant and put it in the box? He had both anyway, didn't he? Sounds like a simple solution to me." I mentally gave myself a pat on the back. I was just learning about all of this yet I came up with a solution my father hadn't thought of.

"Not that simple. The question is, can hope thrive without despair? Will people need to look for hope if there is nothing to cause them pain? Conversely, can despair live on without hope or will humanity implode on itself?"

I shook my head in confusion. We were talking in circles. I swore a thousand marbles were banging around in my head, each with a different question and they were multiplying like rabbits. I looked to Ethan for some sort of simple, black and white explanation but he was still staring at the pendant. "Earth to Ethan." I waved my hand in his face.

Ethan whispered, "So it's true."

"What's true?" Great, another question.

"This is an important piece of jewelry, Samantha," Ethan said. "There's only one Heart of Hope. It can only be passed on to the true descendants of the Angel of Hope. The reason it looks so dull and plain, is that the Heart loses its shine if its owner dies. Your mother died and you've yet to take on full ownership. I'm sure if you try it on, the Heart will begin to shine. It becomes a beacon for the owner. And it heightens the gifts of the wearer. If worn by someone of Light, it will brighten in the presence of poison or darkness. Conversely, if worn by those of Darkness, it will extinguish any hope or faith around it, even that of the one who wears it."

"Wait a minute. If it's passed down from my mother to me, from descendant to descendant of the Angel of Hope as you said, then how can it ever be worn by an Exiled?"

93

Lucas spoke somberly, "Remaining on the side of the Faithful is a choice, Sam. Remember how we told you that we are losing numbers because many of our kind are jumping ship to the Exiled? It's the same principal here. You must choose the side on which you will fight. And the fact that half of your lineage, your father, began in the dark makes your choice that much more difficult."

"You mean because my dad was born into darkness? Why will it be harder for me? I'm not an Exiled, remember? I already know which side I'm on."

With a twinge of sadness in his eyes, Ethan said, "Following the Exiled may not be a conscious choice for you, Sam. There may be too much darkness in you to fight. But if you make the choice to remain Faithful, you've a better chance of fighting off whatever is inside you."

Silent and a bit dumbfounded, I took the pendant from Ethan and turned it over a few times in my hands before I placed it back in the emerald pouch. When I would know it was time to put it on and what I would l do once it was around my neck?

I cast my eyes at a random point on the floor and took a deep breath. "Why would I ever choose them? How could I make that choice? Look at what they did to my family."

Lucas, quiet for a minute, looked at me intently. "Why does anyone, Sam?"

Chapter 6

The next morning at breakfast, the boys decided we needed to leave. They felt the Exiled were getting too close to me. And considering I had the necklace, Ethan thought they would be more apt to look for me there. They weren't sure if Sebastian would know if and when I'd take ownership of it.

After hours spent around the kitchen table, debating where we should go, Lucas determined we should relocate to my father's cabin. "It's perfect," he said. "We can go there, hide from the Exiled while we figure out our next move. Eventually we'll need to find the others, but for now, the cabin is a perfect place to begin her training."

I looked up from the sandwich I was making. "Training? What training?" Wasn't it bad enough they were taking me from my home?

Lucas looked away as Ethan took my hand. "When they decide to come for you, and they will, you need to be ready to fight them."

"The Exiled will come after me." I knew it was true but it didn't make it any less surreal and I had to keep saying it to remind myself it all wasn't just another nightmare.

"Yes. And Sebastian will take this personally." Ethan slipped the butter knife from my hand and began spreading mayo on two more slices of bread. "I wouldn't be surprised if he's the one that comes after you," he said, aiming the knife at me.

"Why is he so bad? I mean, is there a reason he's the leader of the Exiled? What made him choose that path?"

Lucas explained, "Sebastian never had compassion for humans. He embodies everything darkness thrives upon and in return he thrives on everything darkness stands for." Lucas took a bite of the sandwich I'd placed in front of him. "He was angry when God created them. In his mind, angels should control everything including the decisions people made. Then when God gave humans free will, Sebastian went crazy. He questioned God and warned Him that humans shouldn't have control over their own destinies. When God didn't budge, Sebastian did everything he could to undermine God's decision."

"Like Lucifer and the apple?"

"Yes, exactly. Lucifer wasn't working alone, but Sebastian made him the fall guy, so to speak. Over the centuries that followed, Sebastian killed and tortured humans just because he could. And he delighted in it. He wanted all to know that angels were the superior beings. What he failed to realize was that it wasn't our place to interfere.

"Soon he had an army of angels following him and before long, God cast them out of heaven. Many realized they were wrong to question God's authority but by then it was too late. So, they banded together to form the Faithful. They, we, work to atone for the sins of those who fell before us. The others, the Exiled, have taken up with Sebastian's original mission, to do whatever necessary to regain control of what isn't rightfully theirs to begin with."

"Humanity. Free will."

"Right."

"And they need the box and the heart to do that?"

"Yes. Destroying them both will erase any possibility of hope and thus free will. Putting them together will erase any possibility of despair and thus end the Exiled's reign."

"I know I asked this before, but why didn't my dad and mom do just that? They had both. Why didn't they just end it when they had the chance?"

Ethan spoke first. "Because your father knew, as many of us know, one cannot live without the other. There needs to be a balance, if you will. If everything is perfect and there is no sadness, no disappointment, what will be left for anyone to hope for? Free will would be gone as there would no longer be a need to make choices, and God's decree would be broken. Unfortunately, there are still some Faithful who want to erase the Exiled, regardless of the consequences. They don't understand the balance that is needed."

Lucas interrupted. "Both ideas have merit, Ethan."

"We've been through this, Lucas. We've been taught about balance. We've been shown how well everything thrives as long as there is balance. Now that James is gone, another must rise up and take hold of it and not allow the scales to tip in either direction."

My heart sank. "Who's going to do that?"

Ethan squeezed my hand. "If we're right about everything we've learned so far, then you, Sam. You're going to be the one to do that."

***

The following morning, after packing the jeep, we drove out to my father's cabin. It'd been years since I'd been there. I couldn't remember when we'd had the time. And I was going back there, not for fun and relaxation as I once had with my father, but for training and isolation.

Everyday I would train. I would focus on everything they told me. I would do all I could to prepare myself for the one thing I wanted. To face the man…angel…person, whatever, who killed my father. The one who wanted to kill me. I clung to Ethan and Lucas like my life depended on it. And I was certain that it did.

Chapter 7

September
The Cabin

It had been six months since my dad was killed. Even now, I could recall that morning in vivid detail, as well as my dream. Strange, that even six months later that dream was still fresh in my mind. From the intricately carved wooden box and floating script that said *Hope*, to the look on Mac's face as he knelt in front of me. All Mac had to do was look at me and I knew. I knew it in my gut that my dad was gone, even before the words were spoken.

Everyday I wished my dad would come back and that it had all just been part of a sick dream. I went on with my regular routine as I was afraid that if I varied, even a little, he wouldn't be able to find me when he did come back. So even though I couldn't stand the looks of sympathy, I went to school. I went to track practice. I did my homework and hung out with Lucas and Ethan. Then, seemingly without much warning, they had hurried me from my home, from the life I knew, telling me we had to go. Their explanation had terrified me. Perhaps I was in too much shock to comprehend what they were actually telling me at the time.

Even now, it barely seemed real. I almost expected some mornings to wake up in my own house and walk downstairs to see my dad making pancakes or drinking coffee while perusing the newspaper. But that life was over. My dad was dead.

I wouldn't have made it through the last six months if it weren't for them. With Lucas the same age as me and Ethan a year older, I always felt like I had two brothers instead of being an only child. Their father had died a couple of years ago. Like my father, his job frequently took him out of the country so Lucas and Ethan would crash in the extra bedroom or on the living room floor at my house whenever he was gone. I could remember how distraught they were when they learned about the plane crash that had killed him. They huddled in the den with my dad and closed the doors. It was the first time I ever felt left out. It was only recently that I'd been told he was a victim of an exiled attack.

For days afterward, Lucas looked wiped out as strain and exhaustion took over his body. He was tired and sad all the time. Ethan was the quicker of the two to recover. He seemed to understand that, though his father was dead, he would always be near.

Because our fathers had been best friends since childhood, it was only natural that they moved in with us after that. And ever since, we became closer than I thought possible. It was like we could read each other's thoughts. I swore there were times we didn't even need to speak. We just knew. We learned to lean on each other.

When I was younger, I had a small crush on Lucas. I mean, how could I not? However, my feelings for Lucas changed and eventually I no longer minded that he saw me as his kid sister. We had so much in common and understood each other so well we were often mistaken for twins. No matter what happened, I'd always love him. He was my best friend after all. Doesn't everyone love their best friend? Mine just happened to be a guy.

While Lucas and I were best friends, I've never felt as close to Ethan. He was older and always acted like the proper big brother. But not long ago, this strange heated tension developed between us. The love I felt for Lucas was tame and innocent compared to the unadulterated, R-rated lust I began to feel for Ethan. And Lord knew I'd never act on it. But for some reason, whenever he got close, it felt like we were two magnets bouncing off each other. Two negatives or two positives wanting, on some raw, primal level to connect, but we couldn't. Neither of us had shown any obvious interest for each other so it felt like a stalemate. But I was okay with that. I needed time to figure Ethan out because my feelings had me confused.

After my father's death, Ethan had grown more protective, whereas Lucas had become standoffish and authoritative. Ethan was never interested in being 'in charge' and he gladly passed off that responsibility to Lucas. And that completely embarrassing want that I felt when Ethan was around began to grow exponentially. Especially when I saw how he would look at me sometimes and though it was a little disarming, curiosity set up residence in my belly. I couldn't count the number of times he looked as though he was going to say something or act on whatever was brewing between us but he always walked away. I knew Lucas had noticed it too. And since then he had become my shadow. It was odd the way he seemed to not fully trust Ethan, especially since we came here to the cabin.

***

The morning after my heavy training session with Ethan, I woke up still feeling tired and shaken. Nightmares had me tossing and turning all night, while visions of darkness and blood floated around like balloons in my mind. The clock beside my bed smiled wickedly, taunting me. It had only been four hours since I went to bed. Figuring that was all the sleep I was going to manage for the night, I threw off my comforter and swung myself into a sitting position. Rubbing my hands over my face, I willed the visions to find a new host but I knew it wasn't going to happen. As I stretched the sleep and exhaustion from my body, I walked over to the window and pressed my face to the cool glass. It was still too early yet for the sun to start peeking through the trees and the darkness that surrounded the cabin mimicked the dread I couldn't seem to shake. From deep inside, I had this feeling that something was happening. Something was coming. Something bad.

I kept thinking back to the voices I heard whenever I trained. In the beginning, I would only hear the one taunting voice, but now I could swear my dad was trying to break through too. Sometimes it would seem I could hear my dad while I trained and other times, more frequently, I heard a strange mocking whisper that grew louder each time.

I wanted to believe it was my dad who'd helped me yesterday, when the forest began to feel like it was closing in on us, warning me to run. But, the taunts, the warnings, could they both be him? The mocking whisper had always been nondescript and I couldn't recognize it, but could it be? Why would Dad want to taunt me in the first place?

But if it wasn't him, then who was it? Was it the one my dad was warning me about? What exactly was it I was running from? Did Dad know what I was about to face and he didn't want me to face it? If I understood Lucas and Ethan, I was training for precisely the opposite reason. I was training so I didn't have to run.

Thinking about my father brought an all too familiar ache to my chest. A immense, incredible ache that forced me to take several deep breaths. I'd never really known my dad like I thought I did. Lucas and Ethan seemed to know more than I had, yet wasn't I his daughter, his only child? More than that, it hurt that I was never able to say goodbye. The loss had eaten a hole in my heart, a hole that had refused to heal over.

My only solace was that with every piece of me I knew he was the reason I was alive. My dad and Lucas and Ethan had kept me alive. I couldn't let them down. For six months I lived by the mantra, *If its training they want, its training they're going to get.*

With my favorite sweatpants in tatters from yesterday's training session, I pulled on my favorite track pants instead, along with my black DMB Fire

Dancer tee. After throwing my hair into a messy ponytail, I dropped to the floor. I started every morning with push-ups and crunches, but today I really needed to push myself. Making my muscles beg for mercy was the best way I knew to keep my mind off everything else.

After a grueling half-hour, my arms felt like Jell-O but I wasn't done yet. I rolled over and began a 45-minute crunch routine that had me feeling like I was going to hurl. By the end, my abs screamed a litany of curses but I didn't care. My arms, shoulders, and abs shook uncontrollably but I ignored the pain. Still feeling the need for a little push, I grabbed my iPod and made my way down to the training room. I needed to hit something.

Lucas and Ethan had set up a training room in the basement my father had had built when he built the cabin, complete with mat covered floors, full set of weights and a heavy punching bag. I'd been down there many times over the past few months, but never impressed anyone with either my hand-eye coordination or the power behind my punches.

Today, however, I felt like I wanted to beat the hell out of something, so I stepped in front of the heavy bag. Squaring my stance, I visualized the swirling darkness and winged creatures from my dream and began pounding the bag with everything I had. Jabs, uppercuts, backhands, roundhouse kicks…I was destroying this bag. I allowed Rage Against the Machine to dictate my rhythm and it felt amazing. I was Rocky freakin' Balboa, annihilating that Russian dude.

I was amazed at my fluid grace. It was like my body suddenly knew what to do. More pumped up than ever, I pictured the bag fighting back as I jumped, spun, and dove. Catching a glimpse of myself in the mirror, I saw a warrior, not some weak angelic little girl. My skin was slick with sweat and my hair, coming loose from my band, looked darker than normal. I saw muscles I never knew I had gleam in the dim of the overhead light.

I stood for a moment, staring at my reflection, amazed and at the same time confused that I could barely recognize myself. I was cocooned in light and shadow, which seemed to push against each other as if trying to overpower the other. Anger and pride swelled inside me and I became hell bent on destruction. I allowed the darkness to take over as I sent a frenzied flurry of blows at the bag before slumping to the ground with shaky, bloodied hands.

Gone from the mirror was the reflection of the warrior. As I began to cry, I could feel a part of me lifting up and out, until I stood outside myself. From there, I watched the sweat and blood mix and slip down my arms as I sobbed into my hands.

The first time I had an out of body experience was when I was a little girl. I'd been terrified. I didn't understanding what was happening to me. How was it there were two of me? Was I dreaming? Was I dead? When I finally worked up the courage to tell my dad about it, he'd told me not to worry, that lots of people could do it. It wasn't until much later that I realized he'd been wrong, that it wasn't something everyone could do. And it was only recently that I realized I only did it when something bad, or wrong, was happening.

It was strange. I could still feel everything my body felt and knew the thoughts my other self was thinking, but I couldn't say or do anything to interfere. I felt helpless. That was the hardest part, only being able to watch as my other self did or said things I knew I shouldn't or wouldn't.

As I watched, a shallow light began glittering in one corner of the room. In between the pulses of light, I could see the box from my dreams, just as beautiful as I remembered. My other self had noticed it too. The sobbing had stopped and my body was struggling to get across the room to the box. As my body got closer, I was overwhelmed by the odd sense of accomplishment my other self felt and I heard myself begin laughing this weird high-pitched laugh that I knew wasn't my own.

The light coming from the box was so beautiful. A strange awareness of dirty shame overcame me next and I stared blankly as I almost fell to the ground. I wanted to look away. Just as quickly a feeling of point blank defiance surfaced. I could see that defiance like it had solid form. My thinking shifted. *They aren't better than me. Who are they to think so? The box is rightfully mine.* My body maniacally grabbed for the box, only to pull instantly away, my hands singed.

Just as quickly as I had separated, I sank into myself again. I lifted my head and realized the box was no longer there. It never was, I'd been imagining it. My knuckles were bloody and I turned my hands over to see that my palms were covered with bright red blisters. A scream of failure and shame erupted from my throat and I fell to my knees as the room shook and the walls closed in.

It was in this state that Ethan found me. I barely heard him come down the stairs. Without speaking, he crossed the room, sat down beside me and pulled me into his lap. His warmth eased my shaking and he stroked my hair until my moaning became only silently flowing tears. We sat this way, slowly rocking back and forth while he whispered happy thoughts into my ear.

With a flutter, I felt him surround me, pulling me in tighter, and my hands began to heal, the ache in my muscles faded. I snuggled in closer just to listen to the beating of his heart. He tipped my chin and as our eyes met, I could've sworn he was going to kiss me. His blue eyes were narrow with intensity and I felt warmth spread throughout my body. I closed my eyes in anticipation but the kiss never came. Instead, he slowly placed his hands on my eyes and murmured something I couldn't understand.

I awoke in my bed. The sun was peaking through the closed curtains and I rolled over. When I looked at the clock, I bolted upright. Three o'clock. How long had I been out? I didn't remember going back to bed. The last thing I remembered was sitting in the basement with Ethan.

An uncomfortable pit knotted my belly at the thought. He must've thought I was insane. Did I really try to kiss him? More importantly, did he notice and decide not to kiss me back? Mortified, I pulled the covers over my head and counted backwards from one hundred, willing myself not to die from humiliation. What was I thinking? That Ethan would kiss me? That he would want to kiss me? Hadn't I decided I didn't want him to kiss me anyway? I must

113

have lost my mind. He'd never shown anything other than friendly affection and the occasional, harmless flirty comment. What would make me think otherwise? Dumb, dumb, dumb.

I wallowed for a few minutes before I realized I couldn't hide up in my room all day, so I reluctantly forced myself out of bed and into the shower. I got dressed quickly and headed downstairs. Lucas was in the kitchen eating a sandwich.

"Hey, sleepy head! Hungry?"

"Uh, yeah, sure. I'll have whatever you're having."

Whatever he was having turned out to be the most delicious sandwich I ever tasted. Perfectly made, with just the right amount of mayo, juicy tomatoes, crispy bacon and soft white bread, not toasted. My stomach was singing a symphony. I guess I didn't realize how hungry I was until he put the sandwich in front of me.

"So, how're your hands?"

Mouth full of food, I stopped and looked at him. "I think they're fine." Now self-conscious, I tried to turn my body so he couldn't see as I snuck a glance at my unmarred hands. My brain started turning as I took another bite.

What did Ethan tell him? If he told him about the non-kiss, I was going to slip right under this table and hide out for, well, forever. For some reason, other than my own embarrassment, I didn't want Lucas to know. Something about the way I unconsciously pictured Ethan naked at the most inopportune times might explain it. Or the culprit could be the low vibration of want for him that churned in my belly. Regardless, I needed to stop thinking about Ethan that way.

"Ethan told me you were hitting the bags downstairs. He said you were quite a sight. Next time wear gloves."

"Huh?"

"If you wear gloves, you won't beat up your hands. You must've worked out hard 'cause he said you were so tired, you went back to bed. That was hours ago."

So he didn't tell him.

"Ah, yeah. I don't know what I did but I was exhausted. Must've overdone it."

Silently eating my sandwich, I watched as Lucas walked over to the fridge and grabbed two bottles of water and placed one in front of me.

"Look, Samantha…" My eyes rolled involuntarily as I figured he was about to lecture me, yet again, on the importance of training safely. "I know that everything that's been going on the past six months is a lot to take in. If you want, we can just sit on it for a while and revisit any questions you have when you're ready. The history is important but so is the training. So, for now, we'll just amp up the training and go from there. We'll see what we have to work with and we'll talk about what you want to know as we go. Just, no secrets this time. No holding out. Deal?"

"Deal," I said and took a long swallow of water. "Speaking of training, where's Ethan?"

"Oh, he said he had to clear his head so he went running. He left a few hours ago. He'll probably be back soon."

I hadn't realized I had finished the first one, when he placed another sandwich in front of me and told me to eat up. He sat down across from me and watched me for a bit. I knew he wanted to say something else that wouldn't come out. The way he looked at me made me sad. He must have decided that whatever he'd wanted to say wasn't that important because he silently brought his plate to the sink.

He grabbed his keys from the counter and said, "I'll be back in a little while. I've got some errands to run."

"Wait. Lucas?"

"Yeah?"

"Thanks."

"No problem." He paused at the door, opened his mouth to say something, smiled instead and walked away. The jeep roared to life before slowly fading down the road. I was alone.

I finished my sandwich and brought my plate to the sink, rinsed it then loaded it into the dishwasher. Silence had descended throughout the house and a thought popped into my head. Now would be a good time to practice the little trick I'd been working on. I felt silly doing it with Ethan and Lucas around, but now I had the house to myself.

Facing the fridge, I focused and aimed my right palm at the door handle. Envisioning it opening, I pulled my hand back and a squeak escaped my lips as the door mimicked my movement. Staring intently at the second shelf, I willed a bottle of water to come to me. Slowly, it began to shake a bit before flying into my outstretched hand. *Awesome*. Another flick of my wrist had the door closing again. I did a little happy dance. *God, I'm a damn Jedi*. Laughing to myself at the thought, I opened the bottle and took a long swig.

Samannnnnnthaaaa…

I spit out my water and froze. All the hairs on my arms stood at attention as my fight response overtook my instinct to flee. My muscles sang, tensed and ready. My vision hazed and the air began to hum around me. Suddenly, everything inside me knew the voice belonged to Sebastian.

Samannnnnthaaaa...

Unable to speak, I wiped the beads of sweat from my forehead and looked around. I swung my head toward the window and peered outside, searching for the source of the taunting voice. *Where was he?* The sky had darkened significantly and just beyond the trees I saw a swirling shadow that seemed to pulse. The vegetation surrounding it had withered, becoming gray and lifeless as though the shadow had sucked up all of the energy. A faint hum filled the air, growing louder as the shadow pulsed faster.

Samantha. It's time. Join us.

"Where are you?" I could barely get the words out. "What do you want from me?" This voice had plagued me for months and I wanted to know for sure it was Sebastian, yet the thought of finally knowing, finally seeing him, scared me more than the uncertainty.

The voice chuckled.

Join us and I will show you everything.

"Never," I whispered. "Never. My father died protecting me. I will never come to you."

Again, a high-pitched and foul laugh rang in my head, making it spin. Dark clouds rolled ominously overhead, the wind picked up and the dull humming became inescapable white noise.

Silly girl. You will come to us. You will make the choice. It is your destiny.

Despite my protest, I stepped toward the window, then leaning over the sink, I reached up to unlock it. My reflection was unrecognizable in the glass. My hair was wild and my eyes were huge and black as shadows emanated from within me. Whatever was out there was reaching for me with ghostly fingers and as I opened the window, a dark mist snaked toward the house. I closed my eyes in giddy anticipation of the unknown.

"Samantha! Get away from the window!"

I was jolted out of my trance by Ethan's voice. He rushed at me, pushing me out of the way and I fell to the floor hard. He faced the shadow outside and lifted his palms, uttering some sort of chant that sent a stream of light at the swirling shadow. With a thunderous crash, it vanished and the sky brightened once again.

"What were you doing Samantha? What were you thinking?"

"I, I don't…know."

"You don't know?" It was obvious from his tone that he didn't believe me and I instantly felt like a brat who got caught stealing cookies.

"I don't really remember. I don't know what happened, Ethan."

He bent down, offering his hand to help me up off the floor. I'd banged my shoulder pretty hard but the pain wasn't nearly as bad as seeing the hurt in Ethan's eyes. "Are you alright?"

I looked at him with a half-hearted smile as I took his hand and pulled myself to my feet. "Yeah, I think so, though I have a pounding headache now." I rubbed at my temples. "I think it was Sebastian?"

"The Exiled. It's one of Sebastian's followers. They're getting closer. They've been watching so they know your father's protection is wearing off and they can see you're struggling with your choices."

"I'm not struggling! I'm on your side." I threw my hands up in desperation and turned away from him with my shoulders slumped. "What do they want? They told me I had something they need. Is it the pendant? Is it me?"

"Both. You have the pendant so they need you."

"The voice, it asked me to join them and when I refused, it told me I would join them, that it was my destiny. Does that mean the choice has already been made? Why give me a choice when fate has already decided my path?" I wanted to scream. "I told you I'm going to fight with you. I choose light."

With that Ethan sat down, suddenly looking tired. He barely looked me in the eye when he answered. "I don't know what your destiny is. The only thing I can think of, like we told you before, is that your father was an Exiled. His blood flows through your veins. You have both the light of the Faithful and the darkness of the Exiled within you."

"I will never join them, Ethan. Never."

Wary, he replied, "I know, Sam. I know."

Somehow he didn't sound convinced and it scared me. He sighed and patted my shoulder in a half-hearted way before walking upstairs to take a shower, and I was left to the questions circling through my head. When I turned back to stare out the kitchen window, my eyes were drawn toward the spot where the shadows had been. The only evidence that remained was a charred spot on the ground, as though the forest floor had been burned. Placing my palm on the window I closed my eyes and focused. When I opened them, the blackened earth was replaced by lush green grass.

Chapter 8

I was lying on my bed, staring at the ceiling and letting the music drifting from my iPod speaker clear my head when Ethan knocked on my door. At my answer, he walked in, that *I-need-to-say-something-but-can't-figure-out-how* look on his face again. Neither of us spoke as he lay down next to me and stared at the ceiling, too. The silence dragged on as though each of us waited for the other to break the silence.

Time slowly passed as my iPod shuffled my *moody* playlist. Jack Johnson, Van Morrison, Sarah McLachlan and Josh Groban filled the room. As John Mayer began to play, telling us to say what we have to say, I felt Ethan's hand inch over to mine. Our fingers intertwined, palms touching, breathing even, nothing needed to be said.

***

Later, when we all sat down for dinner, the atmosphere felt strained. After Ethan left my room earlier, he'd been avoiding me like the plague. And since Lucas didn't know what went on while he was out, he was obviously confused.

"So, does anyone want to tell me why I'm sitting, having the most uncomfortable dinner in recent memory?"

"It's nothing," Ethan responded.

"Nothing? If it was nothing, then why the silence, curt answers and pushing around food on your plate?" When we didn't respond, Lucas continued, "Okay." He put his fork down and leaned forward. "So, what is it that you don't want to tell me?"

Ethan pushed away from the table, looked at me and said, "It's nothing."

Lucas' gaze shuffled from Ethan to me and I averted my eyes, confused by Ethan's weird back pedal. The grip on my fork threatened to leave marks. I hated feeling like I did something wrong.

"Nothing," I repeated as I, too, walked away from the table. Trudging up to my room and closing the door, I heard Lucas follow up the stairs soon after and walk into Ethan's room. Their voices were muffled but I knew Ethan was quietly filling him in. It was obvious I was not meant to hear this conversation so I sat on the floor by my closed bedroom door and listened anyway.

"The voice told her it was her destiny, Lucas. Like she's meant to become an Exiled. We're grooming her to join the Faithful, but what if we don't have any control over this?" Ethan's voice was shaky with fear as he pleaded with his brother. I could hear him pacing the floor and was sure he was wearing a path in the hardwood.

"Ethan, we knew this was a possibility. With her family history and all, we know her line has spent the majority of their time following the Exiled. All we can do is inform her and educate her about the Faithful and hope she makes the right decision."

"I don't like it. You should've seen her when I walked in. She was saying 'no' but her body was casting a shadow. The air around her was humming. I think it's time we moved her. I think it's time we join the others. Maybe they can help. If we surround ourselves with them, maybe she won't be so impressionable." He sighed and I could picture him rubbing his hands over his face, exasperated.

"You might be right. Her father's protection is wearing off. She's been training and learning faster than we could've hoped but she still has difficulty controlling her gifts. She seems to still be controlled by her emotions. Now that we know what she can do, the others might be able to help us. But, honestly, Sebastian and his followers shouldn't be able to

125

interfere as much as they have been. She should be protected more than this."

"Then let's go! Let's take her from here and go to Jesse where she can be protected in numbers. Where she can be trained by all of us. I feel like at any minute, she's going to slip away and there's nothing any of us can do."

Their voices were muffled by the creaking floorboards of the old house as they continued to pace. I slowly cracked open my door so I could hear them better.

"Ethan, you're going to have to hide your feelings a little better from now on."

"What feelings? What're you talking about?"

"I'm your brother. I know what she means to you. But you can't let that cloud your thinking. One slip and it could all be over."

What was he talking about? What feelings? Could Ethan have feelings for me? That vibe I'd been feeling wasn't just a one-sided hope? My heart jumped at the thought but the poison in Ethan's response interrupted my fantasy.

"You should talk, *brother*. I see the way you look at her. Like you're hungry. The way you're always around her. Always trying to soothe her. Secretly watching her when you think no one is looking."

"Someone has to. Let's just remember whose side you're on. You know it would never work."

Could Lucas see the tension between us?

There was silence for a minute and I swore I could hear a pin drop. I didn't want to hear the rest but I was rooted to the floor. Then the air was filled with anger as Ethan spoke again.

"I was brought to your family as a child, Lucas. I may have been born into darkness but all I've ever known is light. I've been one of the Faithful ever since your father agreed to take me in. I've more than proved myself to you, to everyone. I'm tired of constantly having to show everyone which side I'm on. I've been more of an ally to both of you than you've ever known. Don't you dare throw circumstances that have always been out of my control in my face again."

What? Did I hear that right? I was frozen by Ethan's cold and deliberate words and a cloud of confusion shrouded me. Ethan and Lucas weren't actually brothers? What the hell was going on? Ethan was born an Exiled? What other secrets had they been keeping from me?

"Or what, Ethan?"

"Lucas, use your head. You've no idea what you're insinuating."

"Yeah, well, I just think it's funny how they're getting closer to her. They're getting inside her head, and you never seem to be able to do anything about it when the shit goes down. You don't seem to know how to do your job."

"What're you saying, Lucas?"

"Nothing. Nothing." Exasperation filled Lucas' words. "You're right, let's just get her out of here." He sighed. "This arrangement isn't working. We need to go and be with the others. She needs more of us surrounding her, and you need to keep practicing with her."

Ethan's voice was barely above a whisper when he spoke again. "Well, you do whatever it is you have to do to make this happen. Call whomever you need to. Just get it done, and fast. At the rate we're going, I don't think we have much time."

"Fine. I'll make the arrangements. Just watch yourself with her. Remember, it won't work. It's not *allowed* to work."

With that, Lucas stormed out of the house, leaving me dumbfounded and scared.

"You may as well come out now. I know you heard everything."

Feeling foolish, I slowly made my way down the hall. My legs were like lead. I stepped into Ethan's room, trying not to make eye contact as he

128

sat, defeated on the edge of his bed. I could feel his eyes on me. Not sure what I should do, I tentatively sat down in the worn leather chair in the corner of his room. The air felt thick and I was having trouble catching my breath. It was hard to meet his eyes, but when I did, I noticed they'd changed from his usually brilliant blue to a dull gray.

There was something different about him. About me. The air was electric between us and I felt the usual tension between us building. I could still feel the lingering touch of his hand in mine and I forced myself to relax.

Ethan cleared his throat. "So, Sam. Now you know. I was born an Exiled. Terrible thing, really. But the light is all I've ever known. I just wish he could see that."

"But how? All this time I thought you were brothers."

"Well, we were brought up as brothers. My mother turned away from the Exiled and took me from my father when I was a toddler. The Trotters agreed to protect me and raised me since I can remember. Lucas is actually my cousin. His father is my uncle."

Not knowing what to say, I deliberately walked over and sat beside him on the bed. My stomach was a sudden flurry of want and need and I couldn't get close enough. Despite all that I'd just heard, for the first time in a long time, I felt free. I felt free of the thoughts and visions that had been controlling and clouding my head. I felt free of the what-ifs and uncertainty. All that was certain was that Ethan and I were in that room, alone. I wanted nothing more than to touch him again. Nothing more than to have him touch me again. Thoughts of his lips and his hands filled the room. Our eyes finally met and I knew I was in trouble. And I smiled at the thought.

"So your father was an Exiled and his brother is Lucas' father?"

As I said this, I inched closer to him. I laid my hand on his leg and the temperature rose a few degrees above unbearable. He slowly traced his fingers across my hand and I gripped his jeans so hard my knuckles paled to white.

"Yeah. Dysfunctional, right? My mother, Emily, wanted more for me so she brought me to Jack, my uncle. It would be the last thing she did. My father killed her. I don't know who he is and I've never asked. I don't want to know."

Chapter 9

The next morning, I dropped my gaze to the floor of Ethan's room and focused on a dust bunny that had, apparently, been procreating.

"Listen, Sam. Lucas and I think I should begin telepathy training with you. We know you can do it, or at least accept the thoughts of others because you hear voices all the time now. You and I are going to do a little experiment here. I am going to think of something and I want you to tell me if you can hear me."

"Okay," I said. After all the voices, Lucas' wings, and learning my father was an angel, nothing seemed crazy or far-fetched. "What do I do?"

"Just sit there and try to hear me."

"Okay."

"Ready?"

"Ready." At least I thought I was ready. I sat and waited. I didn't hear anything. I closed my eyes tightly and folded my hands together. After a minute or two I opened one eye and looked at him. "Did you say something?"

Ethan smiled. "Did you hear something?"

"No." Frustrated, I rubbed my palms over my thighs.

"Hmm."

"What'd you say?" I asked.

"Grapefruit."

"Grapefruit?"

"Yeah, grapefruit."

"Why grapefruit? You couldn't think of anything better?"

Playfully shoving my arm, Ethan said, "You try then, if you're so smart."

I looked at him and tried to think of something to say, something much more clever than *grapefruit*. Thoughts sprinted through my brain, each one passing the baton to the next, until I was dizzy.

"Don't try so hard to think of something to say. Just think of something and I'll hear it. And yes, my eyes *are* an amazing shade of blue."

Mortified, my stomach knotted. "You heard that?" I gasped. "Wait! Can you always hear everything I am thinking? Like, everything?"

Then he laughed the old booming Ethan laugh. "Yeah, sure I can! But I don't. I only listen when I think I need to." As he said this, his hand reached up to brush my cheek.

You are so beautiful.

I felt myself flush and my breath hitched but I couldn't move.

"You heard that?"

"Yes," I barely managed to squeak out. I suddenly wanted him to touch me more. All the emotions I felt for Ethan but refused to acknowledge, bounded forward in that moment. My constant struggle became a seemingly distant memory. My vision hazed and the room felt like it was spinning. I knew he felt the same thing because he shifted to face me and placed both hands on my face as though to steady me. His thumb caressed my lips but he hesitated before leaning in.

The last bit of my rationality stuttered in the back of my mind but the rest of my body wasn't listening.

He was having difficulty crossing the imaginary line, too. "Samantha, we shouldn't…" His protest came out weak and unconvincing.

It was like I didn't hear him. My lips softly brushed his and the spark that had always been between us intensified. *More.* The kiss lasted only a second but I could feel the tingle remain long after we separated. In an instant, I knew all the pining I'd ever done over Ethan was real. Uncomfortable but real. I knew we had some sort of chemistry but I didn't know we'd have this need for each other. And now that I knew for certain he felt something more for me as well, it all became, I don't know, easier. I couldn't quite wrap my head around all of it. I quickly stood and looked at Ethan with a mixture of both confusion and excitement.

Holy Jesus. I am in trouble.

A shy smile spread to his eyes. "So Sam, you feel it, too?"

My voice deserted me and all I could do was nod slowly.

Ethan stared at the floor. "We aren't supposed to, you know? You and I aren't supposed to be together. You and Lucas have always been comfortable around each other, like brother and sister. Sometimes I even thought there might be more to it. Because of the fact that you and I have darkness in our past, we aren't supposed to be together. So I've fought it and avoided you. I've tried to distance myself from you but I can't do that anymore. It's too hard. I'm supposed to be stronger than this but I just want to be with you." He was avoiding eye contact. "You're so amazing. And... well, there are other reasons, too."

I still didn't speak. I wanted to say something to ease his anxiety but nothing came out. Defeat clouded his eyes and I was afraid to touch him, though I couldn't quite pinpoint why.

"You should go, Sam. Just forget we kissed. It never happened, okay?"

I stepped in front of him, taking his hands in mine. He flinched. The reaction was so slight, almost imperceptible. My head was suddenly filled with visions of both hope and despair but I wouldn't let go of his hands, no matter what filled my head.

I pulled him up from the bed so he was standing in front of me. Our eyes locked. I could see what he was thinking. I could see everything. His sadness and restraint were so unbearable but still I held tight. Our mouths were barely an inch apart. I slowly reached up, slipping my hand into the hair at the back of his head and pulled him in slightly. He didn't resist. Our lips met again and it was like a thousand lights switched on. Every nerve in my body danced. Every cell in my brain was firing. He kissed me back and I lost all control.

I wrapped my arms around his neck and pulled him in closer. The want became need and I couldn't get enough. I yanked off his shirt and ran my hands down his back, feeling the muscles tighten. The need became hunger, our hands furious as we touch. I grabbed at his belt. This is moving way too quickly but I can't, or won't, stop.

Not here.

We no longer needed to speak to communicate. Our thoughts raced back and forth and we heard what the other is thinking.

I want this.

I was lifted off the floor, our lips locked in frantic exploration.

I know. I want this, too.

I felt weightless in his arms as he carried me down the hall into my bedroom.

We shouldn't.

I know.

He folded me into my bed, my head propped up on the pillow, his body on mine.

I want to.

I know.

Lucas can't know.

He won't.

My hands gripped the sheets as his tongue caressed my neck, slowly unbuttoning my shirt, my jeans. Too slow. I needed him. In frenzy, I pulled his face to mine and push myself into his thoughts.

Ethan...

I know.

His eyes drifted open. He looked at me. His eyes widened as his face filled with shock. He jumped back. "What the... Samantha!"

"What? What is it?"

"Your eyes!"

"What? What about my eyes? What're you talking about?"

"They're not blue anymore, they're black."

That was the last thing I remember before reality hazed away.

Chapter 10

My eyes flashed open. I was lying in my bed wearing only a pink tank top and matching boy shorts, but I didn't remember putting them on. As a matter of fact, I didn't really remember going to bed, but my clock and the sunlight streaming in my window declared it was now morning. What the hell happened last night?

I suddenly felt the ghosts of Ethan's hands on me and I blushed, both from embarrassment and an instant need to see him. I smiled and curled myself under the covers, remembering. My body responded to the memories with a renewed fire in my belly, an insatiable need to feel him again. For him to feel me. Everything about me was different. Electrified and alive. With this renewed energy I got out of bed and changed my clothes.

I pulled my hair back, ready for my morning training when a single memory popped into my head. I stepped in front of the mirror.

My eyes still black, I backed away from the shadow that materialized over my reflection. Why did I feel like I'd done something wrong? Why did I feel like I just stabbed my best friend in the back? What did I do?

I sank to the floor, shaking. What was I thinking? It was then I realized it. For the first time in a long time I wasn't thinking. I didn't consciously think about what I was doing. And it felt amazing to be rid of all the answerless questions that I'd been carrying around. All I remembered was the need I felt. That need turned to greed and I took selfishly.

Oh my God. Did I make a huge mistake? No. No I didn't. My hands began shaking uncontrollably. *What was happening to me?* The pain in my heart was almost unbearable and I had difficulty breathing. My iPod in hand, I ran downstairs and out of the cabin. I needed to clear my head.

Running through the woods usually helped me put things into perspective, especially when it wasn't a training run. No focus needed, no anticipation or anxiety necessary. Early morning runs made room for me to think. The way dewdrops dangled from the leaves and grass and reflected the waning moon mingled with the rising sun always calmed me.

But not then. Nature rejected me. I felt the branches of the trees retreat as I raced past, not wanting to touch me. The sun clouded over and refused to shine. My body struggled to find the rhythm of the usual crunch-crunch of my stride as I raced over fallen leaves. I attempted to organize my thoughts but I only became more confused than ever. How could I have been so selfish? I ran faster. I couldn't shake the feeling that I'd taken something from Ethan. My body tensed. I felt like I was controlling him though I knew that wasn't possible. My hands balled into fists as I pumped my legs faster.

He'd verbalized how he felt. And I'd just stood there staring at him like a mute before I was able to move. I still couldn't believe what happened. I couldn't regret it, though. My head and heart tried to force my body into shame but I just couldn't feel sorry for what happened. Maybe it was supposed to be this way. Maybe I was supposed to be with Ethan. All this time I'd wanted to take the next step but I'd thought there was no chance. That there was no way he could possibly return my feelings.

After an hour in the woods, the sun still hid from me. The woods, usually teeming with morning wildlife was eerily quiet except for the low reverberating hum that began to fill my head. I couldn't shake out the uncomfortable skin-crawling numbness that had taken over, like a million ants were swarming over me. The air suddenly spun around me as a furious anger erupted from within me. Trees bent away and rain fell from the sky. Tears streamed down my face.

I wasn't sure how long I'd been sitting there, in the middle of the woods, but I was no closer to deciding what to do than when I left the house. Calm had long since washed over me so I decided to return.

Roller coaster emotions had become the norm for me. The only time I'd felt sure and in control over the last few months was the night before when I was with Ethan. It was like he woke me up. Or at least that's how it felt that night. I'd felt trapped in the dark and he woke me up, but I was unsure if that feeling would last. There was only one way to find out if this wasn't some broken hallelujah. I had to talk to him. I turned up the music and tuned everything else out.

***

The cabin was still dark and quiet when I crept in. I walked to the kitchen to make myself a bowl of cereal and jumped in surprise. Lucas was sitting at the table drinking coffee. In the dark. Alone.

My heart sank. He knew.

"Morning, Sam."

Okay. I reminded myself to stay calm, maybe he didn't know about Ethan and me. We might've been just friends but who would want their best friend kissing their brother? *Act natural.* I tentatively replied. "Morning. Whatcha doing sitting in the dark?"

He took a casual sip while keeping focus on nothing in particular. It was creepy. "Eh, just too lazy to turn on the lights, I guess. Did Ethan run with you?"

Still unsure, I poured a bowl of Cheerios and sat down at the table with him. I could barely see his face in the darkness. He was hidden in the shadows. If I could just see his eyes, I'd know if he knew. "No. No, I ran by myself."

Sighing, his tone became authoritative. "You know you shouldn't do that. You should have one of us with you. Especially in light of what's been happening."

I paused mid-bite and said, "I know. You're right. I won't do it again."

He leaned forward and I could finally see his eyes. "You okay?"

I couldn't bring myself to look at him. With a nervous chuckle, I answered, "Yeah. Why?"

He reached across the table to touch my cheek and I pulled away. He frowned. "I don't know. You look worried. Pale. Different."

Shit. "Really? Probably just ran too hard. Trying to amp up the training, ya know?"

Great. Now I added liar to the list of grievances against me. I tried to remain calm as I filled my mouth with cereal, hoping I didn't have to say much more.

"Yeah. I know. Listen, Sam. I want to apologize for my behavior yesterday. I was scared. I took most of it out on Ethan. I actually need to talk to him, to square things out. When he wakes up, could you tell him I need to talk to him when I get back?"

"Sure, but where're you going?"

"I'm going into town. Gonna fill the Jeep up with gas and get it ready. We're leaving today."

"Oh. Where're we going?"

"New England. Look, are you sure you're okay? Something feels, I don't know, off, I guess."

Before I fumbled through another non-answer, the lights came on and Ethan walked into the room. A familiar fire kindled in my belly. He just stood there staring at the two of us with a weird look on his face but it disappeared before I could define it.

"Good morning, Sam. Lucas," he said casually as he crossed the kitchen to the coffee maker and began pouring himself a cup of coffee.

I could feel myself heating up. I stole a glance at Ethan and my mind flashed back to last night. *Holy Jesus*, I thought as I pictured skin and sweat and... Stop it, Samantha. Just leave it. I shook my head to chase away the images.

I couldn't see his face because his back was to me but I swore Ethan was smiling.

Are you okay, Sam?

Lucas greeted him, "Good morning."

Yeah. You?

Yup.

I began to choke on my cereal and he chuckled out loud.

I think Lucas knows.

"Ethan, listen. I want to apologize for yesterday. I was out of line."

He doesn't know anything, Sam.

Looking over his mug of coffee, Ethan replied, "Don't worry about it. You were worried. We were both worried. No harm, no foul."

How do you know?

Lucas walked over to Ethan. "I was just telling Sam I was going to go and get the Jeep ready. We should leave today."

I blocked him. He doesn't know.

More confused than ever, but knowing I couldn't show it, I bent my head over my bowl of cereal and shoveled Multi-grain Cheerios into my mouth. A weird feeling surged through my body and I had to force myself to remain seated. Why did I have a terrible and sudden urge to hurt Lucas? I had a desire to tell him what I'd done and watch the pain fill his eyes. I slowly began to stand.

Ethan's eyes pierced mine. *Don't, Sam. Sit down.*

"I agree. I've already let them know we're coming. You get our transportation ready. I can pack us both up. I'll have Sam pack her things. We should be ready to go by mid-afternoon."

"Good. Look, Ethan…"

Ethan responded with a bit more snap in his tone than necessary. "I said, don't worry about it. We wouldn't be *brothers* if we didn't disagree every now and then. Now go. Get things ready on your end. I'll pack up here." I wasn't sure if I was the only one who heard the hint of sarcasm in Ethan's voice when he said 'brothers' but they hugged anyway and Lucas left.

It was just me and Ethan in the cabin now. I couldn't see Ethan's face since he'd turned back toward the window and it troubled me. I sat there and stared at the wall, stunned by the thought that I would want to hurt Lucas that way. I didn't even want to think about it.

"Ethan?"

"Yeah?"

"What did you mean, you 'blocked him'?"

"You know how you and I can communicate without talking? Well, you can do that with him, too. You may not know it or you may not have had the need to do so before, but you can. As can I. So I blocked that moment from him. You and I can 'speak' of it but he can neither hear us nor can he see what we remember. It's best that way."

"Best for him? Or us?"

Sighing, Ethan's shoulders slumped as he replied. "I'm not sure, Sam."

Don't do this, Ethan.

He took a few cocky steps toward me. He looked at me as though this was all just a game.

Don't do what, Sam?

Did he regret it? Did he not feel what I felt? I was barely able to contain myself. I felt possessed, barely able to keep myself from walking over to him and touching him. Had he already brushed me off? *Oh my God.* I looked at him. *You will not walk away from what happened, Ethan.* Mortified at the thoughts that had taken over my brain, I brought my bowl to the sink and rinsed it out. I stiffened as his thoughts intruded mine.

Oh, Sam. I'm not walking away. I can't.

Crap. He could hear every insane thought I had. Every raw, naked, perverse idea that invaded my mind. *Ugh.* Since when had I become such a sex freak?

With a smirk he said, "I can't hear everything. But I did hear that."

Stunned, I dropped the bowl and it shattered in the sink. *Damn.* A shard of porcelain was sticking out of my knuckle. I fought to keep my balance as my knees decided they no longer wanted to support me. Ethan held my wrist, pulled out the shard and kissed the puncture mark. Heat, once again, flowed through my veins and I was dizzy with lust. I could feel him fighting the urge to kiss me. I could hear his thoughts filled with memories of last night. I suddenly felt like I was attached to strings, like some wicked marionette puppet, as I moved closer.

"Look, Sam, I don't know if we should... I mean I was just trying to train you and all. I didn't know it'd get so heavy."

"You've opened the door, Ethan. Don't close it now." I felt like I was watching myself and I felt my heart contract. "Ethan, is this real?"

"I don't know, Samantha. I really don't know."

"But I heard you..."

"You heard Lucas. Last night was a mistake. It had to be. We aren't supposed to be together. It will never work."

148

His words pierced my stomach with fire. "How can you say that?" I never would have allowed anything to happen if I didn't think it was supposed to be. "So what was last night? After all this time you spent avoiding me, what was last night, Ethan?"

"Last night? We kissed. That's all. And what about you, Sam? How about the way you've pined after Lucas since any of us can remember? Like a silly little girl following a puppy. What made you change your mind? Was I some random afterthought? You couldn't get Lucas to notice you so you settled with me?"

The sting of my palm across his face echoed in the now silent kitchen. His eyes, downcast, refused to meet mine. I could see the print of my hand glowing red on the side of his cheek like a painful rash. Anger boiled inside of me and violated every inch of me. I wanted to scream at him, hit him, punch him. None of that would do any good.

"Screw you, Ethan."

I stormed out of the kitchen and pounded up the stairs to my room. How could he be so two-faced? Ten minutes ago he was making jokes and kissing my wounds. Two minutes ago he ripped out what was left of my heart. And there was nothing I could do other than cry myself numb.

Chapter 11

Everything moved quickly after that. I was in my room packing when Lucas came home and he and Ethan began loading up the car. My skin was still humming with anger from my little episode with Ethan earlier and I moved through my room quickly, trying not to forget anything important. All I was allowed to bring was what would fit into my oversized duffle.

New England. I had to pack for cold weather and I pouted a bit at the thought. *Sometimes I really missed Florida.* My bag, now stuffed with sweatshirts and pants and long sleeve t-shirts, was almost ready to bring downstairs. I picked up the emerald jewelry pouch that contained my mom's pendant off the nightstand. After a quick look inside, I resisted the urge to take it out and wear it. Instead, I shoved it into the pocket of a pair of folded jeans that I then crammed into my duffle. I zipped up the bag and called down to the boys that I was ready to go. I grabbed the sweatshirt that I left folded on my bed, put it on and threw my iPod into the front pocket. I slipped my cell phone into the back pocket of my jeans and made my way out to the car.

Ethan decided to drive the first part of the trip. Not that I cared because I couldn't even look at him without wanting to scratch his eyes out. I did my best to make myself comfortable in the backseat. As Lucas walked out of the house and made his way to the Jeep, he stopped suddenly, looking into the woods. When he finally climbed into the passenger's seat, he told us we needed to go.

The trip was pretty uneventful with Lucas and Ethan arguing over who would pick the radio station. After listening to them debate about which band actually started the Grunge movement for what seemed like eternity, I laid down across the backseat. Turning on my iPod, I closed my eyes to Jack Johnson and attempted to let go of all the confusing stuff that happened over the previous twenty-four hours.

My mind was restless, however. On one hand, I was still shaken by the conversation with Ethan that morning. What was wrong with him? My head was buzzing with all the nasty things I wanted to say to him. My stomach turned when I thought about his reaction. How could he be so callous? How could he be such an ass? I felt like I was used and discarded. But then again, I couldn't help the hormonal reaction

I got when I thought of the night before. Though it wasn't like we *did* it. He stopped before we had the chance. He stopped because of me.

I was going insane with confusion but I couldn't let on, however, with Lucas there. Lucas couldn't know what happened. He could never know. Not like it was gonna happen again, that was for sure. I couldn't believe I let him kiss me, touch me. Just thinking about it made me feel like I needed a shower. I'd never felt more stupid. And the longer I focused on that discussion in the kitchen, the more I felt rage building up inside me. The more my skin buzzed with anxiety.

On the other hand, I kept thinking back to what happened the night before. Whatever that was, I was certain it wasn't me. I mean it was me, as in I was there. It just wasn't my personality. I was never forward and I would never in a million years be bold enough to proposition Ethan like that. Hell, a week before, I did all I could to avoid the charged tension between us, as did he. If I didn't know any better, I'd swear I was hypnotized or something but since I could remember every torrid detail, I filed that idea away. I just didn't know what came over me. Whatever it was, I couldn't help but be okay with what happened despite its abrupt ending this morning.

I knew that I was the one who came on to Ethan. I knew I was the one who made the first move. I knew that my behavior was so out of character; I swore I was watching myself on TV. I couldn't even look at him without hot flashes and red cheeks. *Jeez, Samantha, you really stepped in it.* Oddly, I didn't feel the slightest bit of remorse. I felt like I should, though. I'd spent all those years pining after him and he hadn't given me a reason to think he felt anything back until that night and then I ruined it. What the hell had happened to my eyes anyway?

If Lucas knew, he'd never forgive me. Even though his behavior had always leaned toward distant brotherly affection, I knew in my heart he'd be devastated. My skin prickled when I thought of the moment I almost told him. I actually *wanted* to be hurtful. All I could think about in that moment was striking a blow and I knew, somehow, that would be the uppercut that knocked him out. *Since when did I become so careless?* I was torn between feeling bitter betrayal and the hungry greed I still felt for Ethan; the physical and heartfelt amazement at what we'd shared and the feeling of abandonment when Ethan rejected me. Either way, someone was going to get hurt and I had a feeling it wouldn't just be me. I shut my eyes tight and tried to expunge the backstabbing visions from my mind.

On top of everything else was my confusion over the whole telepathy thing. How had I picked that up so fast? Is that why I'd always felt like we could finish each other's sentences? Was it because we really could? Or did I just pick it up that night because there were emotions involved? I had no answer.

Ethan was no help either. I hadn't communicated anything with him other than tense one-word utterances since we'd started our trip. Maybe he'd blocked me as well. The thought made me feel slighted and a little defensive. *Who was he to block me? Who was he to ignore what happened?* Maybe I could figure out on my own how to block him right back.

That thought also deserved to be dumped in the trash. Why did I suddenly feel like I was back in elementary school? Jeez. Obsessive much? But he certainly didn't forget last night. He more than showed how good his memory was this morning. Too bad he remembered it as a mistake. *Stop, Samantha. Stop obsessing. This isn't you! Just leave it. New place. New behavior.* Ugh.

I clung to the hope that maybe he'd change his mind. Maybe I should've been institutionalized for flip-flopping between disgust and anxiety. Maybe he did me a favor. Why would I want to be with someone like that? And what was that whole mess with him saying he was a consolation prize? *What the hell?* Then again, maybe he was right. Maybe I was nothing but a user. Maybe I was the one who hurt him. A bit sad at the thought, I switched to a new playlist. The first song reminded me to break free from the thoughts that clouded my head. *Oh, you have no idea.* I pulled my pillow from the seat next to me, fluffed it up under my head, and willed myself to sleep. Anything to shut down my brain. At that point, I was beginning to think I was going crazy.

I slept fitfully as my mind hazed between scenes of Lucas and Ethan and scenes of darkness and light. In my dreams, I saw Lucas surrounded by light, crying out to me, trying to get to me but he couldn't. I was laughing at him. I was the one pushing him away. With my palms outstretched, I tossed him around like a rag doll. He was fighting to get to me with all he had and I lazily drove him back with every advance. I was cloaked in swirling shadows. No, it wasn't shadows that concealed me. I had wings.

Suddenly, my mind flashed to a foggy vision of Ethan. His eyes were no longer blue. They'd taken on some dark, misty color. We were intertwined in some sort of passionate embrace, though I was trying with all my might to break free. He was laughing and wouldn't let go. With every move to escape his grasp, he pulled me in tighter and the darkness grew around us. I screamed and cried, fighting to no avail. I could see Lucas out of the corner of my eye, on his knees before some black swirl of shadow. I saw the glint of a black sword raised in fury. As it fell, I screamed out and watched helplessly as Lucas crumpled to the floor, bloody wings beside him. The sword rose again and, with one swift movement, it pierced Lucas' chest and the light that once surrounded him faded immediately to nothing.

I awoke in a sweat and looked around. Lucas was driving now and Ethan was asleep in the passenger seat. I shakily sat up, wiped the sweat from my forehead and tried to even my breathing before I dared to speak. "Lucas?"

"Hey. You've been sleeping forever."

"Yeah. What time is it?"

"Midnight."

"Midnight?" *Where are we going again?*

"Yeah. We're almost there. We took the long way in case some of the Exiled realized we were leaving."

"That's a good idea," I said.

My stomach growled. Loudly.

"We picked up a sandwich for you when we stopped. It's in the cooler by your feet."

"Thanks," I muttered as I reached down and searched for it. I unwrapped it and took a bite. *Ham and Swiss.* The familiar combination was strangely comforting.

"So, how've you been over the past few days? It's been pretty hectic and we haven't had time to really hang and talk like we usually do. I've kinda missed it." Lucas turned to look over his shoulder and winked.

Normal Lucas. Normal, happy, sensitive, fun Lucas. No sign of the moody, brooding guy that crashed the party so often lately. God. I felt like an ass. Regardless of what his feelings were or weren't, he'd been my best friend since, like, diapers and I'd been an ass. But he didn't know I'd been an ass and that made me feel much, much worse. I scrunched down in my seat trying, unsuccessfully, to make myself invisible. Lucas kept peering at me in the mirror and smiling. My heart pounded in shame.

"Hey. I have an idea. We have another hour or so before we get there. Why don't we do the lyrics game?"

The lyrics game. I felt nauseous. Lucas and I loved music so much and had been to so many concerts together that we made up a game, which we'd dubbed the lyric game. One of us would sing a few lines from a song and the other one had to name the song title. Ethan had played a few times but I'd lost count of how many times Lucas and I had stayed up till dawn trying to stump each other. The thought made me smile through tiny tears that welled up.

"Sure, Lucas. The lyrics game. You go first."

"Wanna pick the genre?"

"No. You go ahead."

"Ok. Here goes… 'And once outside the undertow, just you and me and nothing more, if not for love I would be drowning…'"

For a split second, my mind raced to the cliffs and ocean water that had plagued my dreams lately. Nausea threatened to overwhelm me. My vision blurred and my ears filled with a distant buzz. Thoughts of my father swam in my brain. I pulled myself out of the thoughts just as quickly as they flashed into my head. My sweat cooled as my skin flushed.

I half smiled. "Going recent this time, huh? I thought you didn't listen to anything that wasn't at least 10 years old."

"You know it? Man, I thought I'd have you with that one."

"Of course, I know it. Only one of the best bands of all time! Pearl Jam – Amongst the Waves."

"Ha-ha. Shoulda known you'd get it. Your turn."

He looked so happy. It was like we were the old Sam and Lucas again. Funny, it felt like we'd been separated a lifetime. But it'd only been a few months.

I thought for a minute, I wanted to pick a good song. One that meant something.

"Ok, slugger… 'In times of trouble, in times of pain, you and I will always remain…'"

His head whipped back but I didn't meet his eyes.

"Sam. What made you think of *that* song? You wrote out the lyrics to this song when my dad died. Remember? You ripped a page out of your notebook at school and taped it inside my locker. Remember?"

"I remember."

In that moment, I was grateful for the night camouflaging the silent tears that streamed down my face.

"Aw, Sam. It's so weird, but over the past few days, I feel like I've lost you or something. Stupid, I know. With all the training and all the stuff we've told you about your dad and family, you've probably just avoided me on purpose. And you've been hanging out with Ethan. I don't know. It just feels like it's been weird."

"I know what you mean. I thought you were avoiding me."

He gave me a look that melted my heart. "I wouldn't do that. I could never do that. I was just a bit freaked out. I'm scared for you."

"Love ya, Lucas."

"Love ya, too, Sam."

It was always the way we said it. *Love ya.* Sighing, I looked out the window and noticed we were, once again, in the woods. *Can't somebody set me down next to a freaking pizza place? A mall? Civilization? Is it really too much to ask?*

"Lucas, where are we?"

"Massachusetts."

"I'm sorry? Why?"

"Well, we had to move you from Florida to the last place and now we needed to come here. There're people here that can help us train you. Together we can help you gain a bit more control over your gifts so the next time you shatter a window, it'll be on purpose."

"Ha-ha. Now you're making jokes. I thought I hurt you."

Laughing, he said, "Sorry. I couldn't help it."

"So, who are we meeting? Are we staying with them?"

"Well, see for yourself."

We turned down a wooded drive. I couldn't see what he was talking about for a minute. Then, suddenly, the woods ended and there, on top of a hill, loomed an old two-story farmhouse. The front porch was expansive and inviting, the shutters were quaint and the front door, much like the rest of the cabin, seemed to hold everything up with strength and the windows were lit up in preparation for our arrival. Regardless of the inviting welcome laid out before me, I'd never been more uncomfortable. My skin started to itch and a headache began to brew. I could barely think of anything other than the fact I had to get the hell out of there but I knew it might be too late for that. And besides, what would I have told everyone? *Sorry, can't stay. This house, though very beautiful, gives me a heavy dose of the heebies.* Call me crazy, *I always do,* but I didn't think that would fly.

The front door opened and two men stepped out onto the wrap-around porch and fixed their stares on the Jeep as we pulled up to the house. Lucas reached over and lightly shook Ethan out of his hibernation.

"Ethan. Wake up. We're here. Sam, we'll get everything from the car in a bit. Let's go up and make our introductions first."

Rubbing sleep from his eyes, Ethan didn't

even look at me before we got out of the car.

The three of us made our way up the walkway to the foot of the stairs. One of the men came down the steps to greet us. In the porch light he looked tall and broad. With his dirty blonde hair, sprinkled with signs of age, and crow-footed blue-green eyes, he gave us the once over before landing on me. I felt like he was looking through me rather than at me, and the feeling intensified the creepiness of the place. I was the first to look away before he spoke. "Ethan, Lucas, Samantha. Welcome. We've been expecting you."

Ethan smiled uncomfortably and reached out stiffly to shake his hand. "Jesse. Thanks for letting us come on such short notice. This is Samantha. The one we've been watching over."

Jesse turned back to me and extended a hand and I gingerly took it, expecting my hand to wither up and fall off. When I met his eyes, all traces of that searching gaze was gone. "Samantha. We've been looking forward to meeting you. We've heard you've had a time of it the past few months. No matter. We'll have you up and ready before the protection wears off. Tomorrow is your eighteenth birthday, right?"

Tomorrow? In all this mess I'd forgotten that my birthday was the following day. Whatever shelter my dad provided me would disappear the moment I turned eighteen. The shock must've been visible on

163

my face and I was sure whatever tomorrow brought hadn't been lost on anyone but me. Ethan's stare bore through the back of my head and I could tell he knew my surprise.

Ethan's face was cast in shadow as Jesse turned to Lucas and hugged him. "Lucas! Lucas! Welcome back, son." All formality had vanished. "It's been too long. Let me look at you. You look more and more like your mother everyday, God rest her."

"Thanks, Jesse. I've missed you, too."

Jesse looked to us, then to the man still standing on the porch. "You two remember my son? Samantha, this is my son Scott. Scott, come down here and greet our guests properly."

Scott was the spitting image of his dad, minus the graying temples. Still boyishly cute while Jesse had that George Clooney distinguished thing going on. He smiled a bit when he shook my hand and hugged Lucas. He nodded at Ethan, all trace of a smile gone. I noticed that Ethan, too, wasn't smiling. Instead, both boys' eyes grew dark as they looked at each other with thinly veiled disgust. I could actually feel the tension rise around me. *Huh. Wonder what that's all about?* Jesse seemed to sense it, too, as he quickly corralled us into the house.

We walked into the foyer and I noticed, off to

the left, what looked to be an office. A desk strewn with papers and a computer faced the door and twin chairs, while a table and ottoman were haphazardly placed in the corner. To the right was the living area with comfortable looking sofa and two massive leather chairs that made up the bulk of the furniture. My stomach sank a bit when I noticed they had no TV. *Seriously?* I suddenly needed to sit down, as I unexpectedly felt spent. As if reading my thoughts, Jesse asked us to have a seat. Then the three of us waited in stiff silence while Lucas and Scott went to the back of the house and reappeared after a few minutes with some drinks.

"So, Samantha," Jesse began. "Ethan tells me you've finally discovered your gifts."

I shifted uncomfortably in my seat. This wasn't the conversation I was prepared for. I wasn't prepared for any conversation at all, when I thought about it. I'd just figured we'd come in, meet and go on with whatever was next. Talking didn't seem to make the list of what to expect. I had the terrible feeling I'd been thrust onto a stage and blinded by the spotlights. I concentrated on my shoes and mumbled a "yes".

"I've been told they're surprisingly strong considering they've only just begun to surface. Please, in your own words, tell me what it is you can do."

My head drew up to meet Jesse's level gaze. I was having trouble with this question and didn't know what to say. I'd been sheltered for the past few months, the only people I'd come in contact with were Ethan and Lucas and now I was expected to spill my life story to a complete stranger? I didn't want to be on display. With a glance at Lucas, he nodded his head and smiled reassuringly.

"Well, I guess I can fix things. I've been practicing breaking twigs and branches and putting them back together. I can also recall objects. I would sit by the water and toss rocks into it. I've been able to sorta pull them back to my hands when I focus."

"Tell him about the kitchen incident," Ethan interrupted with an authoritative tone that I didn't appreciate.

My eyes darted at him with, what I was sure was, thinly veiled irritation. "I got angry one day a few months ago and the kitchen window shattered all over the floor and all over Lucas." At Jesse's look of surprise, I continued quickly, "but I fixed it. I concentrated and was able to restore the window and remove the glass from Lucas. He was bleeding where the glass hit him, but when I fixed it, the cuts were gone, like they never happened."

"A healer." It was Scott's turn to speak.

"You've had no training, yet you were able to fix the window and heal Lucas? You were able to collect yourself enough to do that without hurting anyone? That's interesting."

Now fully unable to get comfortable, I shifted in my seat as my ass tried to doze off. I knew about the whole healer thing, but I was a bit wary discussing it with strangers. I was suddenly acutely aware that all eyes in the room were on me. I never meant to break the glass but I couldn't quite remove the guilt from my conscious.

Jesse looked at me like my dad used to when he was concerned. "Samantha, what did you mean when you said you were angry? Was it simply a matter of happenstance or did you mean to break the window?"

My voice had a bit of force when I replied. "I would never purposefully hurt either Lucas or Ethan. I would never purposefully hurt anyone. I resent the implication."

Whatever spotlight I felt shining on me when we walked in was nothing compared to the microscope I'd now been shoved under. Who were they to assume I would intentionally hurt Lucas? Did they know about what happened with Ethan and I and think that was my fault, too? Did they think I'd used him and forced him to push me away?

167

I needed to get out of there. I needed to leave. I was having a hard time breathing and it felt like the walls were closing in on me. My head spun and I needed air. What must they think of me? Were they judging me, taunting me? *God help me.* I looked around the room to silently convey my desperation when Scott spoke.

"I think you're misunderstanding my father. He doesn't think you would intentionally hurt anyone. The problem, so to speak, seems to be the power of your gifts. Power without training can be dangerous. Without training, the strength of your gifts may increase or decrease depending on the level of emotion you're feeling. It is these emotions we must understand if we are to participate in your training. We need to know what, exactly, we're dealing with."

Dealing with? What am I, some common thug?

As quickly as they came, the thoughts faded. While his choice of words made it sound like I was no more than a pest control problem, there was no accusatory hint in his tone, no judgmental vibe. He didn't think I did it on purpose.

I looked down momentarily at my once-manicured hands and thought back to the kitchen incident. Was it only a few months ago? It felt like a lifetime. "Lucas and Ethan were telling me about my father, what he was and I didn't believe them. I tried to leave the kitchen, but Lucas stood in front of me and I remember him asking me to try to understand. He didn't want me to leave until I'd accepted what they were telling me. I think I said that I would hurt him if he didn't move and that's when the window shattered."

I tried to explain as best I could without sounding like a maniac. I kept replaying the incident over and over in my head since it happened, but I still couldn't figure out what exactly happened. Tears welled up in my eyes and I didn't fight them.

"I didn't mean to, I didn't mean to hurt him. It's just...my dad had just died; I was overhearing discussions about moving me into the middle of nowhere to train for something that, at the time, I didn't know anything about. I was tired. I am tired. My best friend is a freaking angel. How would you feel if your whole life screeched to a halt and then was dismembered by the revelation that your whole life was not what you'd thought? That everything had been a lie?" The longer I rambled the higher my voice got. I seemed to be yelling out explanation after explanation in one long, drawn out sentence. I could feel myself going over the edge, but I just couldn't stop myself. "How could I've not known any of this? Why didn't my dad tell me? Sometimes I feel like I am a zombie; like I don't have control over my own body. Other times I feel more alive than I ever have. And the voices. The voices won't stop…"

I completely lost it then and went all psychiatric patient on them. I curled up into a ball as tight as I could as all the weight of the past few months crashed down. From my dad, to Lucas and Ethan's angelic reality, to betraying Lucas to fighting the hate I should've felt for Ethan after he seemed to so casually cast me aside but couldn't bring myself to hold on to. The training, the physical stress, the constant voices, the dreams, the realization that tomorrow was my eighteenth birthday…I couldn't hold it up anymore. I felt broken and lost and tired. Just so tired. The last thing I remembered was Ethan picking me up and carrying me to bed. And I slept a dreamless sleep for the first time in forever.

Chapter 12

I awoke the next morning as the first light of day fought its way through the heavy curtains in my room. It took a few moments to rcmember where I was, and why we'd come here. I lay still as I allowed my eyes to focus in the waning darkness and my mind raced with thoughts of what was in store for me as I prepared for my father's protection to dissipate. Would it slowly end or would I suddenly have a visible target on my chest? Would I be able to feel this temporary shield leave me? Would it be painless? Whatever it would be, I knew that I felt like I had a stronger bond with my father and I knew I would mourn it when it passed. I didn't know when - an hour from now? Two? At 11:59 that evening? All I knew was that at some point that day I would be a walking bulls-eye.

Mortified that I freaked out like that in front of Jesse and Scott, I pulled the covers over my head. Lucas and Ethan knew me, though a year ago I wasn't the wimpy, cry-at-the-drop-of-a-hat mess that I'd become. Since we'd lived together, in close quarters, for the past six months, they'd grown accustomed to my crazy outbursts of anger, fear and sadness – I called "her" the new Samantha.

I would never in a million years show to strangers what I exhibited last night. A crying train wreck. A sad, sorry, mess of a girl even I had trouble recognizing. I wondered what they thought of me, not that it mattered or would change what happened. But what if it did matter?

Ugh! Again with the wishy-washiness. I was losing control and I wanted to scream.

There were days I felt great and in command of my emotions and physical self. But more and more often, there were other days where I was certainly not in charge of the ship. I did odd, out of character things. Like that whole episode (had it only been two days ago?) with Ethan. What was *that*? I couldn't say it wasn't a welcome distraction, however. And the day I beat the hell out of the heavy bag, what got into my head? And again, the night before, when I broke into a sobbing mess of rollercoaster emotion. I was losing control and I needed to get a grip before I fell off the deep end for good.

I could feel the puffiness of my eyes and I dreaded facing anyone. What should've been a great day, *my* day, would, I feared, probably be the worst of my life.

Shifting in my bed a bit, I heard the muffled

sounds of someone moving around downstairs. Forcing myself to disengage from all my wallowing, I dragged myself out of bed. Not wanting to turn on the light as I felt like I needed a few more minutes of anonymity, I squinted at my surroundings, looking for my duffle and pulled out a pair of cargo pants and a long sleeve t-shirt. My room was freezing and my feet were so cold that I grabbed the thickest socks I owned and slipped a fleece over my t-shirt. Hair brushed and pulled back, boots tied, I no longer had an excuse for moping around in that strange, cold room so I walked downstairs, attempting to prepare my brain for intense who-knows-what.

I moved slowly down the old, creaky stairs trying to adjust my squinty eyes to the dim lights. Still groggy, I meekly walked into the kitchen and found Jesse making breakfast for an army. I remembered for a moment that the house was filled with four men and Jesse prepared food accordingly but the thought of eating anything right now made my stomach revolt. I wasn't sure if I'd even be able to choke down a piece of dry toast. All I wanted was coffee. Black.

"Good morning, Jesse," I mumbled as I walked to the coffee pot, rummaged through the cabinets and looked for a mug.

"Good morning, Sam. How did you sleep?

Was the bed comfortable enough? Were you cold at all?"

Smiling a bit at the fatherly way Jesse voiced his concerns, I managed to croak out, "Everything was great, Jesse. Thank you."

"Can I get you anything? I wasn't sure what you'd eat so I made a few things. Not like any of it will go to waste either. Those boys have huge appetites."

"Coffee would be great to start. I think I need to wake up before I can make a decision between those pancakes and French toast."

Jesse laughed easily as he opened a cabinet, pulled out a mug and poured me a huge steaming cup of coffee that tasted like heaven. I shuffled to the table and watched him busy himself with a few more things before he, too, picked up a cup of coffee and sat down across from me. He was contemplating something and whatever it was, he was taking his time finding the words. Fine with me. The silence wasn't at all uncomfortable considering I had only met this man hours ago and had dissolved into a sobbing, fetal-positioned mess during said meeting. Not the proudest moment, I could assure you.

I should've apologized but I needed to gauge his reaction first. I decided to let the silence envelope us and waited for him to say whatever it was that was on his mind. I was pretty sure I could've waited all day.

It wasn't until we were on our second cup that he finally spoke. "You'll be training with me this morning, Sam. I know you and I've just met but I feel, in this case, it would be better if I were to take over your training for today. I'd like to see what we have to work with. Plus, I'm pretty sure I can answer a few things the boys can't. After today, I think the training will rotate between myself, Scott, Lucas and Ethan. Each of us has a strength that would allow us to, sort of, personalize your instruction. How do you feel about that?"

Somehow I knew he would say something like that so I wasn't at all surprised at his suggestion. "Whatever you think is best, Jesse. I've only just begun to realize what's been going on. I just need to get a hold on all the confusion that's been swirling in my head. Light. Dark. Angels. Hope. Exiled. Faithful. There's so much I don't know, so much I don't understand. I know I was brought here for my safety though. Lucas and Ethan have been so worried; at this point I'd do anything to ease their concerns. Just tell me what you want me to do and I'll try my best to do it."

Seemingly satisfied with my answer, Jesse stood and walked over to the counter. He carried back a huge stack of pancakes and told me to eat up. I still couldn't even fathom eating anything. My stomach was on the defensive but I figured I'd better do as he said since he was in charge of me for the day. The word 'babysitter' popped into my head.

"You'll need the strength," Jesse said. "I'm going up to get ready, we'll be leaving soon and I've already packed sandwiches for us as we won't be home until dinner. Meet you out front in twenty minutes."

I felt like I needed to say something. I didn't want him thinking I was going to fall apart every time something got difficult. I needed to at least put up a front of strength, if not for any other reason than to convince myself. "Jesse, I want to apologize for last night."

"Don't mention it. It's been awhile since we've had crying girls in the house and I don't think it will be the last."

With a wink, he turned away but looked back quickly. "Happy Birthday, Samantha."

He left the room and I sat with nothing but a stack of golden, buttery pancakes to keep me company. Silently singing 'Happy Birthday' to myself, I decided to just go with it as I dug in. Hunger kind of crept up on me and I began eating like an animal. It wasn't until I was rinsing my plate that

Scott strode in. He looked troubled and tired, and he wasn't much for eye contact. If anyone didn't get any sleep, it was certainly Scott. I handed him a cup of coffee and without so much as a thank you, he took it and abruptly walked out of the room. I turned back to the sink and muttered, "You're welcome," sarcastically under my breath when a whispered voice at my ear made me jump and stifle a scream.

"Talking to yourself again? You know that's not healthy."

"God, Ethan. What is it with you? Is it your job in life to make me jump out of my skin?" He was standing so close my heart threatened to beat out of my chest. At least I wasn't getting the silent treatment but then again, maybe I should've been the one giving him icy silence. But I just couldn't. And why did he look so sad?

He laughed uneasily as he reached around me to pick up a mug off the counter, brushing against me as he did. "No. That's not my job. It's funny though." He ducked as I threw a dishtowel at him.

"It's not funny."

"It's a little funny." He was so close I could feel his heart beat. "Happy Birthday, Sam."

How could two people be standing so close without actually touching one another? I forgot I was supposed to be angry with him. Or was it hurt and

177

disappointed? Or was he supposed to be angry with me? For Christ's sake. Now I knew what my dad meant all those times when he talked about teenage girls with their drama and feelings and angst. Oh my God? Was I one of those girls?

I whispered, "Thank you."

"Listen, Sam. Can we talk later? I think I need to explain a few things."

Heart in my throat, I suddenly lacked the ability to speak so I just nodded.

"What's up? How's the birthday girl?" Lucas came in the room and sat down next to Ethan. My eyes threatened to bulge out of my head. How the hell did Ethan get to the table so quickly? And why were my knees suddenly wobbly and unsteady? My heart stopped for a minute and I turned to busy myself with drying my plate.

"Sam is annoyed because Scott is being his usual charming self."

Lucas grinned a bit and told me not to worry about it. Scott was, he assured me, apparently always like that.

"Well, he doesn't have to be rude."

"True. But he is and he will be until he decides not to be. Really, Sam, Lucas is right. Don't worry about it. Anyway, how're you doing? Feeling better at all?"

I couldn't think. I was still unsure of what to do now that Ethan ended his twenty-four hour festival of silence. I had training to do and with my awesome display the night before, I needed Jesse to see that I was ready. I threw the dishtowel on the counter and turned to the boys. "Well, whatever. You two find your own breakfast. Jesse certainly gave you enough choices. I have to get ready. And yes, thanks. I am feeling a little better. I don't know what came over me."

Lucas looked up. "Wait a minute. Get ready for what?"

"Jesse is training me today. We're leaving soon and we won't be back till dinner. So you two, uh, three, are on your own without the grace of my company for today."

"I don't like it," Lucas said. "I don't want you training without one of us there. It's our job to watch over you."

The harshness of his voice made me freeze in my tracks. I turned, slowly, and gave him the once over before I allowed myself to respond, doing my best to keep the sarcasm at bay. "I don't see what the problem is, Lucas. Jesse wants to train me today and then have you guys rotate days. He explained it and it's fine with me."

"He *explained it* to you? Why didn't he

179

explain it to us? I thought I was taking you today. We were supposed to figure this out as a group. He doesn't get to decide. You don't have to go, Sam. You don't have to go if you don't want to."

"Lucas, stop it." I let Lucas hear the annoyance in my voice. "You brought me here because it was safer. You brought me here so we could get help with my training. This was your idea. This was your choice. Jesus. Make a decision and stick with it. I'm going. I'll see you later."

Unreasonably pissed off, I ran upstairs to grab my things. The house was pin-drop silent as I slung my backpack around my shoulders and walked out the front door. Jesse was waiting for me. I wasn't in the mood for idle chitchat so I said, "Let's go," and walked down the drive.

The driveway was long. I hadn't noticed the night before when we arrived or perhaps it only seemed longer now that I was on foot. About a half mile down, Jesse turned off onto a well-worn path that led us into the surrounding woods. The morning sun streamed through the branches and warmed me from the chill of daybreak. Birds in flight and squirrels joyfully digging for nuts seemed to be our only company. Hands in my pockets, I felt the familiarity of my iPod and thought about pulling it out before I quickly nixed the idea. Jesse, after all, didn't know my quirks and I didn't want to insult him by tuning him out. But, then, all I wanted was to tune everyone and everything out of my head.

Damn indecisive Lucas. Indecisive Ethan. Indecisive me. I knew I was being unreasonable in my annoyance but I really was too tired to care anymore. I took a long drink from my water bottle. It was another silent half hour before we changed course.

"Turn left at the stump. We're almost where we need to be. Once we get there, we'll rest before we begin and you can ask me some of your questions."

I quickened my pace, longing, suddenly for answers to questions I hadn't even thought of. Could Jesse really give me straight answers? Could I finally voice the concerns that had plagued my brain over this past year? It could be easier to ask Jesse these things, as I'd so often been too concerned about Lucas and Ethan's feelings that I'd nearly bitten off my tongue in the attempt to silence myself. When it came to the boys, I was either uncharacteristically sheepish and self-conscious or I'd become action oriented, only thinking of the consequences and repercussions after the fact. Again, I thought quickly of Ethan and, just as quickly, pushed him out of my head. The idea that I'd lost the ability to be conscious of the feelings of others had slowly risen in my mind like sunlight piercing through fog.

Samannnnnnthaaaa…

Sebastian's familiar, taunting voice cut through the silence and rendered me paralyzed. My mind went blank save for the notion that I was not safe there and the realization that I may never be safe.

Jesse noticed my sudden inability to move and scanned the woods. "Samantha. What's wrong?"

"The voice. It's followed me here. It's louder here too. Closer than before. It sounds like it's mocking me."

"I didn't hear anything. Are you sure?"

Seriously uncalled-for fury rose in my belly as he questioned me and I glared at him with thinly veiled contempt. *Control, Sam.* "Sure? You aren't seriously asking me if I am making this up, are you? You aren't seriously questioning the sanity I, myself, have questioned over the past six months? If you are, you may as well walk the hell back to the house and leave me to deal with this. I no longer have the patience for piteous glances and furtive whispers behind my back from the people who are closest to me."

I marched ahead in a huff. I was getting so good at those temper tantrums, tantrums that weren't within my control. What the hell was the matter with

182

me?

Clearly taken aback by my sudden outburst, Jesse tried to calm me. "I believe you, Sam. I believe you, I swear. This is neutral territory, so just relax, Sam. Slow your breathing. That's it."

As I looked at him, my consciousness detached from my body again. It was the most surreal feeling and I still wasn't used to it. When I settled outside myself, I noticed something was wrong. Jesse's hands were outstretched defensively and he'd taken a few timid steps back. Odd. Why would he step away from me? I turned from him and came face to face with myself.

I gasped at the sight. My other self was a darker image than the last time. My eyes were blacker than coal and protruded out of my head, like some strange anime cartoon. A huge shadow seemed to emanate from within me. The tension in the air was palpable and pulsed, making the shadow appear oily and slick.

Calm down, Sam. Control, Sam. What is wrong with you, Sam?

I screamed silently at my other self as I tried to slow the boil of turbulence that was creeping up out of nowhere. I'd often been frightened of what I saw when I stepped outside myself but this was horrifying. It wasn't just my eyes, or the air around me, or even my face. Everything about me had transformed. I was completely unrecognizable.

I looked from my other self to Jesse and saw that he was worried as well. No. Not worried, but determined. He had stopped backing away and looked as though he was actually getting ready for battle. I heard myself speak and was mortified at the words that forced their way out. "Look at you, cowering away from me. Sword at the ready, old man?"

Oh my God! What the hell? What was happening to me? I needed somebody get me out of there! Somebody to fix this.

I closed my eyes and tried to picture my life when it was still whole. Before it had started to crumple. Before my dad's death. I dug deep into my memory and pictured myself as a little girl. I was holding my dad's hand and skipping as we laughed to some inside joke that I couldn't quite remember. I didn't know where I was or what I was doing. I just knew that I was happy. Happy that my dad was there to hold my hand whenever I needed it.

Warmth began to spread over me and my hand closed around the phantom hand from my memory. My dad. He was there. And he was smiling.

With my father's help, I calmed down and drifted back into myself. My newfound propensity for flying off the handle was getting out of control. Jesse wasn't the enemy. I took a mental step back, leveling my gaze with Jesse's. As quickly as it happened, it was over. "Jesse?" I stuttered.

"Samantha?"

"I'm so sorry, Jesse. What's happening to me?"

"Your father's protection is ending. It's almost gone."

My eyes welled up with tears and I shut them tight. Hands balled into fists, I repeated over and over in my head: *Daddy, please don't go.*

"I didn't mean to upset you, Samantha. Apparently your emotions aren't within your control yet."

I felt defeated. "I know," I whispered. "Please. Can you tell me, what does it mean for me when you say the protection is fading?"

"The darkness is taking over. Somehow Sebastian has found a way of speaking through you. We need to figure this out before it gets worse and he turns you away from the Faithful."

"Tell me what to do. Please. I will do anything. Just help me. I feel like I am dying inside." Tears rolled down my cheeks. "I don't want this."

Even with my arms wrapped around myself, I was powerless to stop the shaking. Those episodes were becoming more and more frequent. Relief from the malevolence that came along with them eluded me.

Satisfied I was back to myself but still wary, Jesse continued as if trying to convince himself that some freakish out-of-body thing didn't just happen. "They shouldn't be able to come here. You're supposed to be more protected here. We'll have to keep vigilant at least until the others come."

My brain froze. For some reason that news shocked me. "Others? Who else is coming?"

"There are about ten of us, all told. Including, of course, Ethan, Lucas and yourself. . There are many more of us all over the world. We're all coming together to heighten your protection and amp up your training. It was just an idea. Now it seems it was a good one. I didn't know darkness was so prominent within you. I didn't know you'd be so easily manipulated. We'll have to work on securing you emotionally as you seem physically capable. In that respect, at least, I feel the training will be easy."

I felt ashamed and embarrassed and tired. I was tired of fighting the rising evil within me. I could feel it all the time though I hadn't been able to pinpoint what it was, exactly, I'd been feeling. Now I knew it was darkness. The word *manipulated* looped in my head like a broken record. More and more I felt like I belonged anywhere but there.

"I'm not one of them, you know. I don't belong with the Exiled. I'm here, with you, with the Faithful. I want to be of Light. I don't want this shadow clinging to me anymore."

"No, Sam. You're not but it's still in you. It will always be in you. I remember your father having to fight against it when he came to the Faithful. It was hard for him. I fear it will be harder for you."

I lifted my head. "You knew my father?"

Jesse made himself comfortable leaning against an old oak. "James? Yes. He and I were friends."

"How come I never met you? I thought I knew all my father's friends. I don't remember ever meeting you. Then again, I thought I knew a lot more than what I actually do. Everything I thought I knew just, well, isn't."

"We met once, when you were a baby. I was at the hospital when your mother died. She was an angel too, in case you were wondering. And beautiful. She was such a beautiful person, inside and out. Unfortunately, an Exiled attacked her in her sleep."

Jesse paused as he seemed to be remembering back to when it all happened. Sadness veiled his face momentarily before he continued.

"Well, when she died, your father almost lost it. He almost went back to the Exiled after that. It

187

took a few of us to keep him calm enough to see reason. Then he saw you. And all trace of anger and darkness disappeared. He loved you instantly. You were everything and because of that, he kept us away from you."

"But why? Was he angry at you?"

"No, no. Nothing like that. He just wanted to keep the two worlds separate for as long as he could. He didn't want you to find out about all this until you were ready."

"I don't understand how my father died if he was an angel. Lucas and Ethan tried to explain it but it still doesn't make sense. Is there only one way for an angel to die?"

"In order for an angel to die, their wings must be removed and the sword of another angel must pierce their heart. Sebastian did just that. He attacked your father from behind, stripped him of his wings and stabbed him in his heart."

I closed my eyes against the grisly images that infiltrated my brain. Sebastian, the angel that had killed my grandfather. "And this Sebastian, is the leader of the Exiled?" "Sebastian is temptation. He is the devil on the your shoulder, if you will. If Lucifer was the snake, then Sebastian was the apple. His darkness gets inside and eats away all hope, all faith, all love. His main purpose is to bring as many as he can into the depths of despair, humans and Faithful alike. He is smooth and takes the form of whatever pleases the eye of his target. He looks different to all who see him. In reality, he is a demon angel, one that will never be forgiven. His sins are too great and the pleasure he takes from the pain of others is sickening. He will force you to fall in love with him then stab you between the eyes."

What would Sebastian look like when I saw him? For some reason, it seemed certain that I would, before too long, come face to face with my father's murderer. "Lucas said the Exiled shouldn't have been able to come to me when we were at the cabin but they were there. And now they're here too. I still can't figure out who or whatever the hell 'they' are. Dark Angels, Exiled, Boogey Men…I don't care. I only know they've come back. They've found me again. I thought I would be safe here. How do they even know where I am? How is it that they can find me so easily?"

"Today is the day they've been waiting for. Your father can no longer shield you from them. I don't know why they were able to find you before today, though."

"Am I safe?"

"You *are* safe here. Though it's highly unusual for them to seek you out here, with us around you, it's not improbable. I don't know how they've managed to find you so quickly. Your father's protection should've been able to protect you more than this. Until we figure that out, we'll have to be careful. We'll have to keep you safe. It is our fate just as it's yours."

I felt naked and exposed. Like fate was on my heels, a persistent, snarling dog. A thought pushed forward. A thought I couldn't fight. What if darkness was my fate? Sadness and anxiety for all those who were giving up so much to protect me fell upon my shoulders. I wondered if they should've been protecting themselves *from* me instead.

"I don't fully understand this whole good angel/bad angel thing. Can you explain it for me? Lucas and Ethan told me all angels are fallen? Is that true?"

"Sort of. I think they meant all Exiled and all Faithful. We are of the original Fallen, our lineage progressing with help from humans. When Satan fell, he only took a third of the heavenly angels with him. You have to know, there are many different types of angels, from Seraphim, who are the closest to God to Virtues, which, by the way was the type of angel your father was, to archangels who are the guardians of all humanity and angels, guardian angels, who guard over individuals.

"Most of the Faithful would be best compared to archangels. It is our duty to atone for the sins of the Fallen by keeping humanity safe from the Exiled. We continue to repent because, one day, we may be forgiven and allowed to enter Heaven once again. The Exiled, on the other hand, are demons, though they were at one time angels. Many take human form and revel in the sins of humans, even promoting it."

I chewed this over in my head for a few minutes. It was a lot to take in. I didn't know how I would ever keep this all straight. All I could picture was good guys and bad guys. Questions flooded through and I carefully chose the next one to ask. "Can an angel be hurt? I mean, like, injured?"

"Yes. We can bleed, we can break. But we have an amazing ability to heal ourselves. You, being a healer, can ease our pain faster than we can on our own, like you did with Lucas. He could've healed himself, it just would've taken him longer to do so. If our wings are removed but we're spared the sword to the heart, we can heal." He picked up a stick and started turning it between his fingers. "Wings take a long time to heal, to regrow. But they will regrow. Our gifts will be diminished until they regenerate fully but when they do we are often stronger than we were before. Only by both cutting off the wings and piercing the heart will an angel die."

I closed my eyes for a moment to take in all he was saying. There was just so much information, I wasn't sure I was going to be able to learn everything, understand everything before I had to face Sebastian and the rest of the Exiled. "Do all of you have wings? Ethan and Lucas said not all do."

"Yes and no. Many wait years before they appear."

"How do you kill an angel with no wings?"

"Ahhh…If an angel hasn't gotten their wings yet, they must be beheaded." My mind raced to Ethan and I had to choke down the bile that filled my throat.

"Why don't you all get your wings at the same time? Like a right of passage? Like puberty?"

"We aren't sure why. I can surmise it has to do with purity of lineage, either those who have remained Faithful or those who have remained Exiled. We have the ability, you see, to choose on which side we are to remain. Many Faithful fled to the arms of the Exiled because they thought it was easier." He turned his head to a group of squirrels rummaging for acorns. "It is so much easier to give in to temptation than it is to shy away from it. Remaining Faithful is difficult, primarily because you have to believe in hope. Without it, the Exiled will rule."

"Hope? Isn't that where I come in? The box?

The pendant? Is that why I am important?"

Jesse chose his words carefully and proceeded slowly. "The Box of Hope is not unlike the myth of Pandora's box. In it should lay all the sins and troubles of the world. Many years ago, followers of the Exiled forced the box open and let loose a litany of evil and hate and despair. It is, you see, easier to promote hate and sadness than it is to promote happiness and love. The world became as it is now, full of war and gluttony and deceit."

"And the Heart of Hope?"

"The Heart of Hope, once laid into the box will remove the most evil of evils, the most hateful of hate from the world and lock them up within the Box of Hope. Most of us, Faithful and Exiled alike, understand there needs to be a balance. There needs to be sadness in order for there to be hope. There needs to be difficulty in order for there to be faith. At times, even though we have different agendas, we can find ways to get along together. Unfortunately, what Sebastian, and the Exiled that have pledged themselves to him, have done is plague humankind with troubles from which they cannot escape."

"Surely, there are still good people, hopeful people, faithful people in the world?"

"Of course there are, Samantha. But it's getting too easy to drop everything and run for individual satisfaction."

"So, where do I come in?"

"You are a Virtue, you are the one who protects hope. The guardian of the pendant, as your mother was. It is your duty to find the box and lay the Heart of Hope within it to end this fight. However, because the darkness is within you, if you choose to follow the Exiled, you also have the unfortunate responsibility to return it to Sebastian and his followers. That is the war that wages within you. You have to decide. We can only teach you so much, train you so much. In the end, we can only place faith in the fact that you will do what is right. Your choices will decide the balance, or imbalance, of what is to be."

Scared didn't begin to cover what I felt in that moment. Overwhelmed, unworthy, challenged, determined, conflicted - that might've covered a third of it. If I was hearing him right, I was in charge of saving the world and all humanity from self-destructing. But I was just me, a girl thrown into all of this, a girl who'd rather stay ignorant to what was going on around her. How could I have ever been concerned with designer labels, hair and fashion trends, or what kind of car daddy was gonna buy me? For a second, I felt ashamed of the fact I'd rather be in calculus than saving the world.

"You said that 'most' Faithful are archangels. My dad, wasn't though? He was a Virtue?"

"Yes, he was. A healer, a protector. Virtues often take human form as doctors, nurses, scientists, artist, musicians and such. Ethan however is neither a virtue nor an archangel."

"What is he? A demon?"

Jesse laughed at my apparently funny question, but I was totally serious. "No, Sam. Ethan is a guardian angel. To be more specific, your guardian angel. It is his duty now that he has chosen the Faithful over his Exiled lineage. Above all, it is his duty to protect a member of the Faithful, regardless of his feelings for them."

"Feelings?" How did Jesse know about that?

"Yes, Sam. Feelings. He thinks he cannot properly protect one he loves so much. That is one of the reasons you're here. He feels he isn't able to keep you as safe as he should."

My bug-eyed, gaping mouth stare said it all. Was that why it would never work? Was that what they were talking about? Was that why he seemed so quick to back away? No wonder. I felt like a total jerk now.

Chapter 13

We ate a silent lunch, though once again my appetite had dissipated. Jesse, comfortable with me and the conversation we just had, decided it was time to move on. We walked another half hour into the woods until we came to a seaside cliff. Below the water was churning restlessly. I felt like I'd been there before, that the place meant something. I was sure of it but I couldn't figure out what. The edge was rocky and crumbly, daring anyone to step closer to the void. It was both beautiful and frightening.

"So, Jesse. You've brought me out here. Explained that I am destined to either save the world or end it. What's next?"

"We're going to clear your head first, then do some simple exercises. From what I understand, your gifts have shown themselves and you can do amazing things. We need to make sure you can focus on those gifts and control them. In order to do that, you need to be in control of your emotions and you aren't. You are, pardon me, a bit of a mess right now. I'd like to help clean up that mess before I allow training with the others to go on. We may mop this up today; it may take longer. We'll see."

"I'm that obvious, huh?"

"Yeah. A bit," Jesse said as he smiled that fatherly smile of his. I didn't know what it was about him but there seemed to be something familiar in his demeanor. Something about him eased me, calmed me.

"Okay. Clear my head, huh? How do I do that? Is there some sort of angel mumbo jumbo I need to chant or something?"

Jesse chuckled. "No, no. Nothing like that. We just talk for now."

"Talk? That's it? Haven't we been doing that? What are we supposed to talk about?"

"What do you want to tell me?"

Well, wasn't that the loaded question of the century? What did I want to tell him? Was he a shrink now? I was struggling a bit with the truth. Not so much that I wanted to lie to him, as I was sure that would've gotten us nowhere. And I had a weird feeling he'd know if I wasn't being straight with him. I just didn't know how much to tell him. Was I supposed to I tell him about Ethan? Was I supposed to talk about the voices? Did I tell him about the dark thoughts that crept into my head at night? About feeling like I was balancing between some walking zombie and the real me? Thoughts struggled furiously in my head and I almost wanted to shut them out. Instinctively, my hand gripped my iPod. If I could just escape, I would've been able to ignore my way through all the uncertainty that was now, sadly, my life.

I knew he could see I was stalling but he made no gesture to speed the process up. Half of me was relieved at his patience but the other half was begging for a leading question. He didn't say anything though. He was all about me purging at my own pace, in my own time. I knew I had to say something, anything, just to get the ball rolling so I figured I might as well start talking. I sat on a rock, closed my eyes and remembered.

"When Dad died, I didn't know what to do. My mom, as you know, died in childbirth, or so I thought until a few minutes ago, so it was just us, just Dad and me. I know he was gone a lot but not really until I could fend for myself. I guess he was gone more than usual that last year or two. But I had Lucas and Ethan with me so I didn't mind too much. They moved in when their dad died five years ago. It was easy, natural. We'd always been close so there was no real issue with it. I had school, friends, and sports. Then one morning my dad was dead. No warning at all. It was like someone dropped a bomb. Well, not really *no* warning. I did have the dream the night before. I was told he was killed while transporting medical supplies. But now I know the truth. Now I know Sebastian murdered him."

"Can you tell me about the dream, Sam?"

I hated remembering the dream. I hated talking about it. I hated the fact that it kept cropping up. But I told him all about it, just as he asked. I got lost for a minute in the memory. It felt like only moments had passes since that dream changed my life into a living nightmare.

Jesse put his hand on my shoulder to encourage me to continue. "After that, I used a knife to open the paper, because I didn't want to tear it," I said. "But I cut my hand. I don't really know what happened after that. I know, in the dream, I passed out. I know I had a weird vision of my dad. The one Lucas told you about. It was like a dream within a dream, if that makes any sense. Every night for weeks, I'd have the dream. I was stressed and sad and confused and then the incident with the kitchen window happened. That's when I found out Lucas and Ethan were angels, when I saw Lucas had wings. That's when they told me my dad was an angel too. The next day, the morning after I found out about them, Lucas and Ethan took me away. They said it wasn't safe to stay there. They told me it had to do with the box and my dad but I didn't understand. We just left and they took me to the cabin."

"I know it probably upset you, but that was smart of them. Then what happened?"

He watched and waited for me to answer as I stepped closer to the edge of the cliff.

"Once we left and got settled, they started my training. At the time I was too numb to question anything so I did what they asked. I trained to fight. But fight what? At the time I wasn't sure. I didn't understand, I still don't, not really. I just knew that it was something I had to do, to fight the ones who killed my dad. But nothing was clear.

"I can run, fast. I can see three, four, five moves ahead. It wasn't long after we arrived at the cabin that I began to hear the voices more clearly. I began to understand they weren't just tricks of my imagination or me just hearing things. They were actual voices. Sometimes I know it's my dad. Sometimes the voice is unfamiliar to me, yet at the same time it's familiar. I mean, I hear it so often that I've become accustomed to it, but I still don't know whose voice it is. I can only assume its Sebastian or one of his followers. Sometimes I dream of angels and light and darkness. Sometimes I hear weird noises."

Jesse stood next to me, trying to comfort me with his presence. "It seems to me you know a lot.

When they took you away, were you frightened? Did you try to contact someone?"

"No. Who was I going to call? I have no family other than my dad and I wasn't going to call any of my friends from school, though I am sure I could have. Lucas and Ethan were with me. They'd be who I would've called anyway. I mean, sure, I was frightened but I was mostly just sad."

"What is it about *this* place that frightens you?"

Wow. I did not see that coming. How did he know this place was familiar to me? How did he know it gave me the jitters? I needed to work on my poker face, for sure. Time to play dumb. "This place? What do you mean?"

"Samantha, you know what I mean. I saw your eyes. I saw you tense up. I know you've seen this place before. It's why I brought you here."

Okay. Now I was getting the creeps. How did he know? I didn't even know. How would he know the exact location of my vision, if that's really what it was? I wasn't even sure this was the same place.

No. I knew. I knew the moment I stepped out of the brush onto this rocky clearing. I just wasn't willing to admit it. "How did you know?"

"I can read your fears. It's *my* gift. I can read the fears of others as well. Lucas' gift is one of protection. Knowing the exact moment when he will be needed. Ethan can communicate through telepathy. He can also block others from intruding in on thoughts. Scott's gift is his ability to move about undetected. Your father's gift was the ability to control the movement of objects with his mind."

Trying desperately not to believe, I responded sarcastically. "Sounds like we could put together an amazing side show act."

His patience had no limits. "This isn't a joke. I wish it were. I wish you could remain ignorant about all of this but we can't let that happen. You need to be informed if you're to make a decision. You see, Samantha, we know you have the gifts your father had. We know you can communicate seamlessly, much like Ethan. Sure we all can speak in that manner but not as easily and not without oceans of training. In addition, you can heal. There hasn't been a healer, other than your father and Ethan, in a hundred years. And we now know, though you may not know this, you can move about undetected. We aren't sure if it's a conscious thing, an emotional thing or an accident. But we know you can do it. Now we just have to figure out a way for you to do it on purpose."

"What do you mean? How would someone not know I'm there? How would I not be aware of

203

it?"

"This morning, when I was making breakfast, I could sense your presence. Then I couldn't. Then you were right there in front of me. Ethan and Lucas have mentioned instances as well."

I was totally confused. "What instances? They never told me."

"They didn't tell you because they didn't want to freak you out. They weren't sure at first but after the incident in the kitchen, they knew. You see, when all that was happening, you weren't there. Sure, you were there physically so they could see you but your presence was gone. If they hadn't been staring at you, they'd have had no idea you were in the room."

I squatted down and rubbed my hands over my face. This was all too much. "I am so tired, Jesse, of people keeping things from me. Wouldn't it be easier if everything were laid out on the table for me to digest as a whole rather than in tiny morsels of half-truths and partial information? And what does this mean? I have all these freaky super-human - pardon me - non-human gifts, as you like to call them. What does that mean for me? And why does it matter if I have a few cool, but admittedly terrifying, angel-type traits? Isn't that a good thing?"

"Yes. It would be a good thing for us. A good thing *if* you were Faithful completely. But as of yet, you remain conflicted. And we aren't quite sure how all this will play out."

A sneaky blanket of criticism covered me but I knew Jesse wouldn't do that. I was too quick to snap. "What do you mean? I told you I am not one of them."

"You did. I want to believe you but I've seen too many Faithful turn; too many without your gifts, without your propensity towards dark emotions. We'll just have to wait and see." He squeezed my shoulder gently. "For now, however, we must get to some training exercises. We'll finish our conversation another time. Today we'll work on controlling your emotions with your mind. And soon you'll begin sword training…"

"I'm sorry, sword training?"

"Yes. Sword training. If you have to kill an Exiled, you must first cut off their wings. And you can't do that with an ordinary kitchen knife. Why do you think I was explaining all that?"

"Honestly? I wasn't really thinking anything. There was no real visual behind it."

He must've seen the look of utter horror on my face because he added a wink and a chuckle. I knew I was training to defeat the Exiled but for some reason that never translated into 'Hey Samantha, don't forget to chop off the wings of the evil bad guys.' I was so not ready for this. So totally not ready.

"Hey Jesse, before we continue, may I ask a question?"

"Sure."

"Are you sure I am ready for this?"

"I hope so, Sam.

Hope so? Great. What the hell did that mean? Why couldn't anyone just give me a straight answer? Why couldn't they all just spit it out? All I knew was that I was some gifted human training to annihilate some bad guys - scratch that – Exiled demon creatures, with some sword I hadn't learned how to use, or even possessed for that matter, all the while trying to decide where my heart lay. Oh yeah, and Jesse *hoped so.*

Jesse interrupted my thoughts, asking me to move closer to the edge of the cliff. And I really didn't want to do that either. Not so great with heights. I was beginning to think that even though this might've been all about me, it wasn't in the "all-about-me" way that I wanted it to be.

"What do you want me to do?"

"Just step close to the edge and clear your head. Look straight out onto the horizon. Just relax and empty your head."

"Empty my head? Easier said than done, my friend."

"I know. Just try. We may not get this right today but you're so far advanced without training, concerning your gifts, that I thought we might take a stab at it."

"Take a stab at what? What is it, exactly, that you want me to do?"

"Right now I just want you to step closer to the edge and clear your head. Easy enough, right? Simple enough."

I looked at him like he had bananas growing out of his head but I did as he asked. I stepped slowly to the edge and the tips of my boots were about an inch from disaster. I could feel the eroded stone beneath me and watched as a few stray pebbles tumbled recklessly down the cliff. The water was so insane, it was almost hypnotizing. I watched it pull back then throw itself onto the rocks like some child banging their head into a wall because Santa forgot his favorite toy. There was no beginning and no end to the churning mess that lay fifty yards below me. The only things that seemed to make sense were the jagged finger-like rocks reaching from the coastline, like they were put there for a purpose. As I imagined them reaching for me, I quietly reach out too.

"Now, Samantha," Jesse said quietly. "I want you to look straight ahead at the horizon. Let the sun heat you through. Let the line haze. Once you've focused, close your eyes and imagine yourself floating there. Just imagine yourself floating among the clouds. When you've done that, imagine yourself pulling the water to you. Imagine the water reaching up to touch your fingertips."

Who did he think I was? Moses? Seriously. Floating on clouds and pulling water to me? *Okay, crazy pants.* I figured it couldn't hurt too much to do as he asked, no matter how insane it sounded. It was just my imagination anyway, right? I squared my shoulders, not because I had to, but because that was how I imagined I should stand - shoulders squared, feet shoulder width apart, arms hanging loosely at my sides.

Now, I had to toss off the random thoughts that permeated my head. I looked to the horizon. I saw far away flashes of light and dark twisting in some exotic dance. Patchy gray clouds strolled along beams of pale yellow sun. This was all so familiar, like déjà vu. If only I could just place it. The fog was lifting and a crisp view was coming into focus. The sun warmed me through and I felt like I could reach out and touch the golden rays. I closed my eyes and saw myself out there, walking along those sunbeams and strolling through the clouds. My body relaxed and I no longer felt attached to it. As if knowing how all along, I pushed my palms down toward the water

208

and slowly lifted them so they were outstretched at my sides.

I closed my fist gently and brought it to my face as I slowly opened my eyes. My hand crept open and a swirl of water was floating in my palm. I stared at the sphere for a minute. As the sun fell upon my upturned face and I felt its heat, the water warmed up in my hand to the point I could barely stand it. But as soon as I thought it was too hot, it quickly began to cool. It didn't take long before the water form a large ball of ice and I crushed it in my hand. I was floating feet away from the cliff.

Suddenly a burst of uncomfortably warm air whipped around me and I heard a roar erupt from below. Everything around me vibrated with purpose. I didn't know what was going on and I lost my concentration. My insides felt like they were going to melt, the pain was nearly unbearable. I screamed for Jesse but he couldn't hear me.

God, it hurt! I screamed like some tortured animal on the brink of death. The water around me began to hiss as it reached boiling temperatures. I reached out for Jesse and caught his eye. He was scared. I could see he was scared and that he had no idea how to help me. It frightened me more to think he was there but unable to help.

Suddenly, I felt something solid and heavy

209

and hot grip my legs. Like a hand. I looked down and the jagged rocks from below had reached up into the air and grabbed me. They coiled up my legs and wrapped around my body, squeezing me to death. They were trying to pull me down into the chasm below. I felt my skin singe and every nerve scream in terror. I fought the scorching, ever-tightening grip with all the physicality I could muster. But nothing I did eased its deadly grip.

"Samantha!" I heard Jesse scream over the din of boiling water and crushing rock, "Focus Samantha! You can beat this! Go into yourself and beat this!"

Tired and in pain, all I wanted to do was lay down and die. I forced myself to step outside and survey the situation. This was the first time I'd been able to willingly. Head tilted in amazement, I could see my body being consumed by the rock formation and surrounded with steaming hot salt water from the sea below. My skin was red and my body seemed to have given up fighting and collapsed in defeat. I actually looked dead.

Jesse was still on the cliff's edge. His eyes were closed and his arms were stretched toward me as though he thought I was dead too. I could hear him calling to me but he wasn't scream out loud, I mused. He must be doing that telepathy thing. If he could reach me then I could reach back. If he could still communicate with me then perhaps whatever had taken over wasn't invincible.

The situation was getting dire; my body was bleeding and blistered. I could see the blue blush of bruises creeping over every exposed inch of my body that hadn't been touched by the blazing hot rocks. Something inside me told me I could fight it.

I knew I had to fight it.

Focus, Samantha. Just focus on beating this. Beating them.

I looked behind me. Dad! Seeing his face reassured me that I could do it. I stretched my arms out toward my limp body and moved my hands as if I were grabbing the rock and tearing it away. I focused and concentrated and slowly the stone began to fall away. I needed to wake myself up. I stepped back into myself and called up all the internal focus and mediation I could muster. If I couldn't beat this thing physically, I was going to beat it mentally.

Groggy but awake, I ignored the bone deep ache in my body and used my free hand to reach out into the water that surrounded me, screaming out as new blisters blanketed the bruises. Tears mingled with steam. I told myself to think cold. I forced myself to think about my father. I thought about Lucas and Ethan and all the sacrifices that had been made for my sake. I couldn't let all that go to waste. I couldn't let it all be for nothing.

The air around me began to crackle. The rock continued to loosen its grip. I had to destroy it. Reduce it to rubble. I had to destroy the evil that had taken hold of me. Darkness overwhelmed me and I screamed. I screamed in pain, in pleasure; in defeat, in triumph; in hope, in despair. And the world around me exploded with a scream that ripped from my throat and moved the earth like an earthquake.

A calm drenched me. Everything was suddenly quiet and still. It should've felt weird but I knew this was how it was supposed to be. I looked around and time seemed to have stopped. The world was on pause. The water was gone; my earthen prison had disappeared. Jesse was standing next to me. He was smiling, but his eyes were fearful and anxiously amazed. And then I realized he wasn't standing at all. He was floating. I was floating, high above the water.

In my hand was a heaviness I couldn't place. A weight I couldn't shake. My gaze slowly fell down my blistered and bloody arm to my shaking hand. My now glassy vision fixated on what I found. Clenched in my hand was a sword made of ice and rock; formed from the angry water and jagged earth that lay below. I felt loopy. My mind refused to focus and I could barely form coherent words. I wasn't able to see straight and I knew I was fading.

"What the…what the hell is this?" My voice sounded charred and heavy.

Jesse put his hand slowly to his mouth and stared in awe, "My God…A sword. Your sword. I didn't think you would be ready for it. I didn't think it would come to you so quickly. But that means they're closer than ever and more prepared than we anticipated. It also means you're more capable than we thought."

"Is that…is that a good thing?" God, I was tired.

"Good? About you being capable, yes. About them being more prepared, no."

None of this was making sense to me. What was he talking about? "But I…I thought I was just practicing my focus. You said the sword stuff would come later."

"I thought so, too, Samantha. Nothing is going the way it's supposed to. We thought you were too close to darkness to be prepared to fight it now. I think we may have been wrong about that. We need to go back to the house. Now."

Back on solid ground, I tried to walk but pain pierced my body. Jesse offered me his sweatshirt since my fleece had been burned clean through and underneath, my stomach, sides and back had taken the worst of the burn. The skin was charred almost black.

213

Blisters had formed and blood was oozing from everywhere. But at the same time, I could feel my body beginning to heal itself. I was surprised I hadn't passed out already but I couldn't seem to lose consciousness, no matter how hard I tried.

As my brain desperately tried to shut down, I flashed back to my dream. The winged girl, my dad...

The thought distracted me from my pain-induced, weakened state like a jolt of caffeine. I studied my surroundings then quickly sifted and scanned through visions and memories to find the one I needed. "Wait, Jesse. I *have* been here before."

"What? Sam, we need to go. I need to get you back to Ethan." When I didn't move, his face softened. "Okay. You'll be able to focus on healing yourself better if your mind is clear. Just relax and tell me what you remember."

"I—I don't remember the woods, but I do remember the cliff. This cliff. It was high and rocky, just like I remember and the sea was angry. My dad was here and the girl was here, too. There were lights dancing off in the distance..."

I had to pause a minute to work through the pain that felt like it was tearing my skin off, chunk by chunk. I found a flat rock and sat down gently, pushing my head between my knees until the pain induced nausea passed before I continued. "I

214

remember the ground began to crumble at my feet as if I was supposed to fall into the crashing waves. I heard that hum, that buzzing sound."

"There were lights and a buzzing sound?"

I gingerly walked over to the edge of the cliff and peered into the calm waves. "Yes. A weird noise that sounded, at first, like a low hum but as the sky darkened and the wind picked up, the noise became deafening. It was everywhere around me. Within me. I thought I would die from the sound. I heard it again just before we came here. There was something following Ethan and me in the woods. The noise was terrible."

"So, this is where it is to happen," I heard Jesse murmur.

"Where what is to happen?"

"The fight, Samantha. They're going to try to take you here. That or something of importance is to occur here. That must've been what just happened."

"Sebastian and his followers? Here?" I looked around. "When? How?"

"Yes. Sebastian. I don't know when and I don't know how. I just know where. Right here is where the battle will take place." He held his hand out to me. "Now, again, we must go."

Panic pumped through me. Why was I here if they were coming for me? How did I know it

215

wouldn't be right then? I looked down at the sword in my hand. How did I know anything? "Jesse?"

"Yes?"

"I'm scared."

"Me too, Sam. Me too."

Chapter 14

The walk back was almost unbearable. Jesse held me up the best he could for most of the trip. Although my wounds were healing at a faster-than-human rate, it was still excruciating whenever he touched me. Neither of us spoke of what happened. Time, for now, provided a blanket of quiet. The look of amazement that refused to leave his eyes pierced me. I replayed the incident over and over again in my mind as we struggled home but I could make neither heads nor tails of what, exactly, transpired. I was bruised, battered and blistered. But I was safe. For the time being.

These weird out of body experiences were draining me faster than they used to and they were lasting longer than before. I had watched myself being attacked by rocks and water and wind. I felt myself burning. And in the middle of it, was my father, standing behind me as I floated high above the water.

His voice gave me the strength to battle what was attacking me and somehow, someway, I was able to release myself from the claws of earth. As my body healed and the pain slowly faded, my memory became more and more hazy. I barely remembered anything but ice and heat. And somehow I'd come away with a sword. A sword make of rock and seawater. A sword I would use to fight in a battle. A battle between darkness and light, good and evil. The only question was which side would I choose?

I knew which side I should be on, but I had a sinking feeling, it wasn't the side I would end up on. I saw my own betrayal. I saw my anger overtaking me and I was scared. Scared to death.

We stepped out of the forest's shadows and into the waning rays of sunlight. I had no idea what time it was. I was just happy we were finally back at the house. My clothes were torn, my skin looked as if someone set fire to me, blood had dried everything stiff and dirty and from the pain that persisted in my chest I was sure I had cracked a rib or two. I felt as though I would fall down at any given moment and I welcomed oblivion to take me.

Suddenly, Ethan tore out of the house and ran directly to me, his eyes searching mine. "What the hell! Samantha…" *Are you all right?*

Do I look all right?

What happened?

Not now.

Sam…

I said not now, Ethan. We'll talk later.

Concern filled his eyes. "But the sword."

Limping away, I left both Jesse and Ethan behind. I didn't feel the slightest bit of remorse for shunning Ethan's concern. I needed rest and time. Time to gather my thoughts and digest everything Jesse told me, about angels and demons and good and evil. The last thing I wanted to do was talk about anything that just happened. Let Jesse tell the story for now and I'd open my mouth when I felt I should. Right now, I just wanted something familiar and comforting. I wanted my dad.

As I sluggishly walked up the stairs to my new room, I breathed a sigh of relief when I didn't bump into Lucas or Scott. I closed my door, locked it and did everything I could to avoid my reflection in the mirror. I didn't want to look.

Heaviness weighed on my right arm and I realized I was still carrying the sword. *What the hell was I supposed to do with this?* So not in the mood deal with it, I quickly shoved it under my bed before easing down into the plush chair that looked as though it might have once belonged to someone old and comfortable, with a tacky sense of style.

The adrenaline that had carried me home was quickly receding. I curled up in the chair and finally allowed myself to feel all of the bruises and blisters. It was only then that I realized I was crying. I wasn't sure how long the tears had been seeping from my eyes but I had a feeling they were visible when Ethan ran out of the house to greet me.

Ethan. What was I going to do about him? My guardian angel. How was that possible? He was always, until my dad died, so removed from me; always there but distant. It's probably what he had to do and that made what we shared a mistake. I wondered if there was some punishment waiting for him if anyone ever found out about our kiss and the fact that we almost... *I can't think about that right now.* Everything was telling me I was on a one-destination course with destruction.

Totally uncomfortable, I moved from the chair to my bed and sprawled out on top of the comforter. I allowed myself to really cry, not just streaming unconscious tears. I cried in pain and fear. I cried for memories and the unknown. I let it all out with a giant, sloppy waterfall of tears. All I wanted was for Ethan to hold my hand, to hold me in his arms, to kiss the pain away but I knew that would only make things worse. I needed to show everyone I could handle this without help.

My body tingled and my skin stun as my mind floated randomly from subject to subject, from thought to thought. All I wanted to do was sleep, but my brain wouldn't shut up and my nerves refused to stop dancing. I allowed myself one more moment of stretched out relaxation before I forced myself to get out of the bed. I needed something to do, to distract myself. The pain had subsided and I was feeling antsy.

Absentmindedly, I began to unpack my things, to make this room my own. The first thing I unpacked was my iPod speaker. I pulled my iPod out of my pocket, plugged it in and hit shuffle. I needed something, anything to ease my brain so I could think. I let the music permeate my surroundings and I began to feel a calm I hadn't felt in awhile. I found some relief in unpacking my duffle, in refolding my clothes, in organizing my closet.

As I grabbed the last pair of jeans from the bottom of my duffle, I heard something hit the floor. Looking down at my feet I found the pouch that held my mother's necklace. Despite my aches and pains, I bent down to retrieve it. I stared, fixated, at the pouch for a moment or two before I opened it slowly and poured the necklace into the palm of my hand. Silent tears fell as I walked to my mirror.

My mother. There was so much I wanted to ask her. If only I could've had a minute, just one minute with my mom. I wanted to see her face, hug her and hold her for even a moment.

In the mirror, I got my first glimpse of what

Ethan must've seen when Jesse and I had returned. Dried blood, blisters and bruises covered my reflection. My hair was tangled and caked with dirt and seawater. My clothes were torn and the skin underneath, though healing more rapidly than it should have, was still a red-hot mess while my eyes were slowly fading from black to blue.

Shaking my head, I tried to pull out of the empty feeling that had washed over me. I readjusted my ponytail and held the necklace in my hand a bit longer before slipping the chain over my head. The moment it fell into place, the history of the fallen flashed through my head like it had just been downloaded. I saw the pain, the suffering, the brief moments of calm, and the destruction. I saw their fall. I saw the Exiled rise and the Faithful cower. I saw their punishment and their hope for redemption. I saw myself betrayed by a faceless entity that was strangely familiar.

It was too much.

I grabbed at the necklace and tried to take it off but it wouldn't budge. It began to glow bright white. A flash of black was all I saw before I lost awareness.

At some point in the night I woke up, fully clothed and sprawled out on my back diagonal across my bed. My wounds had healed over, leaving no scars. The searing pain was gone. I was left with only a few lingering dull aches and pains. The necklace was closed in my fist.

Funny, I didn't remember taking it off. I didn't even remember getting into bed. I really needed to start dealing with my exhaustion *before* it overtook me, as it had on so many occasions. It seemed I was always running myself until I passed out.

I remembered putting the necklace on and seeing the flashes of the Fallen's history then, nothing. I woke up here on my bed, fully clothed and without wearing the necklace. I rubbed my hands over my face and groaned. I was nowhere near rested but also far from sleep. The rumbling in my stomach reminded me that I hadn't eaten dinner yet, not to mention I'd barely had any lunch. I changed into my pajamas. I figured no one would question a pajama-clad girl on her way for a late night snack. Positive there was a good chance everyone was sleeping, I braved the trip to the kitchen and whatever leftovers, if any, the boys hadn't eaten. The closer I got to the kitchen, the louder my stomach growled. If I didn't eat something soon, there was a good chance it would turn on me.

How had I become a hungry, confused angel - person - thing that teetered on the edge of light and dark while trying to save the world? I rolled my eyes.

223

My life was getting ever more complicated. Lost in my random thoughts, I made my way into the kitchen, realizing too late that I'd walked in on a suddenly hushed conversation.

Jesse was talking with three people I'd never seen before. The first was tall and gangly. As he eyed me, I noticed his face was scarred and broken. I couldn't suppress the gasp as my hand flew to my mouth. He was mesmerizingly hideous and I stared too long and too hard. I forced myself to look away.

The second stranger was a girl, about my age. She was the most beautiful girl I'd ever seen, but she didn't look like she should be. She was all hair. Her hair was crayon black. Black like freshly laid asphalt. She had the fairest skin, almost translucent and pale violet eyes spaced a bit too far apart. Her features were small but prominent against her slight frame and barely visible beneath all the hair. She had an otherworldly aura that promised strength, and I couldn't stop staring.

"Ahem," Jesse cleared his throat before I was able to embarrass myself any further.

"Ah, hi. I was just coming down to get something to eat." Tongue-tied, I was pretty sure that all came out as one word.

"You did miss dinner. Ethan made up a plate of leftovers for you. It's in the fridge." I nodded and attempted to quickstep over to the refrigerator but Jesse interrupted. "Before that, Sam, please come over here and meet our guests. Sam, this is Branna, Cal and Noah. Friends, this is Samantha."

Branna and Cal each nodded their intrigued but distant greeting. The third, Noah, turned and locked his stare right at me.

As if I wasn't already embarrassed to be meeting complete strangers in my pajamas, at that point I felt like I might keel over from the flush I could feel creeping up from my toes. Noah was freaking beautiful. He was about Ethan's height, wore beat up old jeans, a ratty t-shirt and a leather jacket he had to have borrowed from James Dean. My gawking, however, was extinguished by the intense disgust he threw my way.

He was boring a hole into my brain with obvious distrust. He was judging me while I stood there in my pajamas, staring at him. I was being weighed and measured and clearly found lacking. For what, I wasn't sure unless Jesse had already described our afternoon of torture and horror. All I could do was act as though I was clueless. Pretend I was oblivious to the fact that he looked as though he wanted to kill me. I mean, who was he to judge me? He didn't even know me. If he wanted to judge me, I was gonna give him something to judge first.

All in that second, I felt one of my tantrums coming on. I felt the fire in my eyes and my skin was tingling for a fight. *Calm down, Samantha.* That new mantra really was getting old. And it wasn't working. The air around me danced a bit and my vision hazed over. A roar of venom boiled inside me and I prepared for confrontation. With my hands clenched into fists, I felt Jesse wrap his arms around me and heard him whisper, "He's a friend." Only then could I calm myself. Only then did my vision clear. Only then did his hatred dissipate to mere loathing.

"You weren't kidding, Jesse. She needs control," Cal said.

A raspy Irish brogue permeated the air. "We may not have time for her to practice that control, Cal." The voice was Branna's. I certainly wasn't expecting that. I guess my image of red haired, green eyed, freckled leprechauns was way off base.

"I understand that, Branna, but we need to work with her in what little time we have. Even a small amount of focus could help her."

I was about to butt in, to remind everyone that I was still here, when Noah voiced his concerns with a full dose of animosity. "Cal is right, Branna. She is unfocused and dangerous in her current state. Especially with what has happened, she needs the direction now. We must know on which side she is to fight."

On which side? What? *Wait a minute*. Now it was my turn. I was angry and offended and I didn't bother keeping it out of my voice. "Hold on a minute, everyone. Stop treating me like I'm some ticking time bomb. I know I need focus. I know I need to control whatever it is that keeps rearing its ugly head. But if you think I'm going to just stand here while you all talk about me like I'm not even in the room, and look at me like I'm some abomination, you certainly have another thing coming. I know I can get control of my focus. I'll be ready to fight. I've been fine with Lucas and Ethan for the past six months and I've only been here a day and a half. Jesus. Cut me some slack. And I would appreciate it if you wouldn't assume that you'd be fighting against me. I know what side I'm on. The question is, do you?"

Noah looked as though he was about to eviscerate me with some ugly diatribe but Cal saved me from the verbal lashing. "You certainly are a bit feisty, Samantha. You should know what it is you speak of before you let the words fall out of your mouth. And as for 'fine with Lucas and Ethan', you don't seem to have the control necessary to resist the Exiled." He stepped to me and pointed his finger inches from my face. Your outbursts of negative emotion invite them, call to them, side with them. I

227

do not trust you. I think you are a loose end that needs to be cut off. You are dangerous to yourself and everyone around you."

I defiantly looked him square in the eye. "You have no idea who I am. You know nothing about me. Maybe it's you who should know what it is you speak of. I don't need you. I didn't ask for you. I don't want you here."

At that, Cal let loose an ugly laugh that matched the scars on his face. "You are correct in your statements, Samantha. The only difference is we have proven to the Faithful on which side our allegiance lies. You, on the other hand, seem to bounce between the two sides with your emotional responses almost like you are deciding which shirt to wear. You are close to the darkness. Closer than any of us have been. You are all at once intriguing and frightening. We aren't sure what to make of you. You are not yet trusted enough to be called a friend, there is too much darkness peeking through you. As for me, and I cannot speak for either Noah or Branna, I knew your father. He was a good man. Though he came from the Exiled, he did not teeter on edge as you do. He was resolute in his decision to join the Faithful. Because of your father, I am alive and I am bound to do what I can to help you. But, in light of recent events, I do believe we must move more quickly than you could be ready for."

"That's the second time that's been mentioned. If you're talking about what happened with Jesse and me at the cliff today, I know that was bad. But I need the opportunity to redeem myself. He told me things I didn't know, things I was afraid of."

Jesse looked at me with sorrow in his eyes. "It isn't that of which we speak, Samantha. While you were up in your room, we began patrols as discussed earlier. We need to guard this house now more than ever."

I rubbed my hands over my face to contain the massive headache that was about to intrude. "Patrols? I don't remember talking about that."

"We're pairing up to patrol the woods and property to make sure the Exiled haven't come."

"I don't understand what the big deal is, then. Isn't this the safest place for me to be? You said I was safe here. Did you find something? Are they closer than we thought?"

It was Branna's turn to speak, her voice full of anxiety. "They are closer than we thought but it isn't what we found. It's what we can't find."

"What? What's missing?"

"It isn't actually *what* that is missing, Samantha…"

Just then, Ethan walked into the kitchen, a

silver sword strapped to his back. He looked more serious than I'd ever seen him. Something was definitely on his mind; he didn't even glance in my direction. With him were Scott and two more people I hadn't met yet.

"Jesse, we can't find him. We've looked everywhere. And He hasn't contacted us yet. Have you heard anything from him?"

It felt like my stare was tearing layers away from the back of Ethan's head. I couldn't read him but he did turn and look at me with surprise. I could only assume he hadn't realized I was standing there.

"Who can't you find?"

His eyes turned soft for a moment as he searched my face. All traces of the disagreement we had were gone. I searched his eyes for the words I knew were coming but didn't want to face.

"Ethan. Who can't you find?" I repeated.

"Sam, I am so sorry."

"Who, Ethan? Who?"

"Please, sit down, Sam."

Don't say it. Don't say it. "I don't want to sit down. Just tell me."

I am sorry, Sam.

Ethan, who? I silently asked though I already knew the answer.

"Sam, Lucas is missing."

230

Chapter 15

"Missing?" I could feel myself begin to hyperventilate. "What exactly do you mean by 'missing'?"

Ethan took my hand but I barely felt his touch. He walked me to the kitchen table and sat me down. I was only slightly aware of him fetching a glass of water, bringing it to the table and handing it to me. I lifted the glass to my lips and drank as if on autopilot. I barely noticed when Ethan settled in the chair next to me and turned my chair to face his. I was only slightly aware of the fact that I was forcing myself to breathe.

Lucas is missing. Lucas is missing. The words looped in my head, kicking in my gut with every repetition and I couldn't get away from them. Bricks filled my chest and I felt like I was going to break apart from the weight. The hollowed out section of my heart that I'd kept secret was about to cave in on itself and consume me.

Lucas was missing.

"Samantha. Look at me. Sam. Samantha, please look at me." Ethan was holding my hands in his and rubbing them with his thumbs. I looked everywhere but at him. The kitchen was crowded and filled with tension. I saw Jesse and Scott standing together. I saw Branna and Cal looking at me with justified worry. I saw Noah looking everywhere but at me. And I saw the two other people that came in with Ethan. I didn't know them but they looked nice enough. One even kinda smiled at me. They were holding hands and I wondered if they were married. They certainly looked like a married couple or, at least I thought they looked like a married couple. Wouldn't it be nice to be married? Wouldn't it be nice to love someone so much that you'd want to spend the rest of your life with them?

I'd spent everyday of my life with Lucas. We'd held hands, we'd smiled at each other but never in a million years had I thought about what it would be like to spend the rest of my life with him.

Not so with Ethan. The minute he kissed me, I saw a forever I yearned for.

As all those thoughts were whipping through my brain, I knew I was going crazy. I knew that whatever control I was supposed to "focus" on was running from me. I knew that the moment Ethan let go of my hands, all hell was going to break loose and I was going to become the storm. *Breathe, Samantha.*

His voice was easy. "Samantha."

Slowly, I dared to look Ethan in the eye. I could tell he was aware of the simmer beneath my surface. He, too, could see the danger about to explode from within me while he did his best to calm me down. But deep down, I knew his effort is futile. I felt nothing but revenge, cold and desperate.

"Samantha, listen to me. Lucas has gone missing. We are doing our best to find him. We will find him. I am sure he's fine. We just have to find him. You need to relax. Breathe for a minute and listen to me. We. Will. Find. Him."

I was barely able to croak out, "How?"

"We'll figure it out. Together. We'll all figure it out and we'll all find him."

Though my stomach was rolling and it felt like someone had punched me in the chest, I forced myself to pay attention, to not give into the raw instincts that had washed over me. I needed to listen. I needed to hold on. "What happened? When did this happen? How did this happen?"

"Lucas and Scott were first on patrol. After the incident this afternoon at the cliff, we all decided it was best to begin the patrols now. You were up in your room and we thought it best to leave you to your thoughts. I'm sure you were exhausted and confused.

"After Lucas and Scott went out, the others showed up and we began planning what our next move was to be. When Mara, Christian and myself went out to relieve them of guard duty, we found Scott unconscious and bleeding."

I turned to look at Scott. Funny. I hadn't noticed that he looked like a rock had been thrown at his face. Maybe it would fix his attitude.

God, what was wrong with me? The guy was in obvious physical and emotional pain and all I could do was think of how he may have deserved the attack.

Too bad I wasn't the one to ruin his smug face.

"We brought him back here. He explained that he and Lucas were attacked. He has no recollection of what happened to Lucas. Just that they were attacked and he woke up when we arrived."

Not only was I trying to wrap my head around the fact that Lucas was missing; I was trying to control the growing urge I had to wreak havoc on anything and everything around me. And, simmering just below all that chaos was the very real ache I had for Ethan. After being deprived of his closeness for several days, my very real need and want for him was being provoked.

Lucas was my brother. I was going find him and would destroy anything that got in my way, no matter the cost. A heavy weight lifted from my shoulders as if the matter was the last important matter in the world. But at that moment, I needed Ethan to hold my hands and look me in the eye and tell me it would all be okay. If he couldn't tell me that, then I may as well have been as lost as Lucas.

"Samantha, we will do all we can to find him." Branna's voice was soft. "We need you to continue as you were with your training."

"Are you assuming that I'm going to just sit here quietly while Lucas is out there somewhere? Possibly hurt? Possibly dead?" From somewhere a nasty laugh escaped from my lips. "You don't know me very well."

"Samantha," Ethan interrupted quickly, trying to keep his voice calm. "You have to do what they say for now. It's best that you work hard so that we can find Lucas. You maybe the only thing we have that will help us."

"What am I? A map? Can I miraculously locate him? If so, tell me how."

"It isn't a matter of you locating him, dear," Mara said. "With your focus and control of the gifts you have shown and those we think are still cloaked, we think you can lead us to Sebastian himself. If we are correct, not only will we find Lucas, we will destroy Sebastian."

"You want to use me as bait. Fine. Let's do it."

Ethan jumped, "Samantha…"

"No, Ethan," I tried to reassure him. "It's fine. This is my fate, right? Isn't that what everyone's been telling me? I'm going to have to face him sometime. Why not now?"

Mara continued, "He has led the Exiled to such strength that we have not been able to defeat them. We win a few battles here and there but they are winning the war. The only weakness of those Dark followers is that they have but one leader. That leader is Sebastian. If we destroy him, we conquer the Exiled and all the Dark followers."

Ethan pleaded, "Do you see? Do you see how we need you to stay calm? Samantha, you may be the only way we can win this and get Lucas back in one piece." His voice trembled at the mention of Lucas's name. The storm inside me began to quiet to a dull roar and I nodded slightly.

"So, what you are saying is that no one has any idea what happened to Lucas." I timidly voiced my concerns, careful to avoid any inflection that would alert them to the fury that was fighting to unleash itself. "All we know is that he was there and then he was gone. Do we have any idea of what might have happened? Does Scott remember anything?"

"No. He doesn't," Jesse interjected. "We don't know anything for sure. We can surmise that he was

236

taken by the Exiled. We still aren't sure if Sebastian himself has finally arrived. If he has, then it is imperative that we continue with your training while we make our plans. Not only will it help you with control and focus, but once the plan is in place, we can use you in the search."

"Can't he speak for himself?" I sounded like a maniac.

Scott answered defensively. "I can. I don't know what happened, Samantha. He and I went out to begin patrols. The next thing I know, he's gone and my face was bashed in. And I don't like the tone you're using. I don't like the insinuation. Get control before you kill us all. Or is that your plan?"

At that moment I bowed down to the darkness inside me and allowed it to overtake me. I jumped up, stretching out my arms with a sickening wail as the whole room ripped apart. Light bulbs flashed and shattered, windows caved in, tables and chairs slammed against the wall and in the middle of it all was me. I couldn't stop it.

The opening of wings and drawing of swords was barely audible over the deadly ruckus. Everyone was on the floor, except for Ethan who was the only one not looking at me like I needed to be taken down. He was thinking. Alarm bells were ringing in his head and he had no idea I could hear them. If he did, he wouldn't have look so calm. He put his hands up to hold back those that had started to stand in offense and moved slowly to face me. Large black tears fell and stained my face but he didn't look away in fear like before, instead he held my gaze with a steady, calming courage. Eyes dark and dangerous, hair flying, like Medusa's snakes, and white as freshly fallen snow, I could barely bring myself to meet his stare. And even then I had to tamp the contempt in my face.

"Samantha, look at me. It's Ethan. You don't have to do this. This isn't your fault. This isn't you. I know you. I know what's inside you and it isn't this. This isn't who you are meant to be."

I backed away from him. I was scared because this destruction was all mine. I couldn't blame it on an outside me. I was still whole and completely disturbed. Branna was standing, sword in hand, waiting for my next move. I lazily flicked my wrist and the sword clanked to the floor. I turned and saw Noah step toward me. With a look I sent him flying back ten feet. They'd all retreated a bit and I knew they were trying to communicate with each other silently. I held up a hand and the room filled with the deafening buzz that'd plagued me the last few months. I watched them all, one by one, fall to their knees, ears covered in protest. I walked over to Ethan and held my hands over his ears so he didn't have to suffer.

Reaching up and gently brushing my hair from my eyes, he cupped my face in his hands and touched his lips to mine. The chaos ceased to stir, the hum silenced and light filled the room. My rage slowly receded and my vision cleared. He looked like everything an angel should be. Every instinct in my body wanted me to hate him for it. His blue eyes pooled to infinity and for a moment I allowed myself to get lost in them. Something fought against the control that slowly returned and I was left, standing in the middle of the kitchen with Ethan, with destruction all around me. Unable to speak, I mouthed, "Help me," and collapsed in his arms.

He lowered me to the floor and though I was conscious, I was unable to move. My arms and legs had become heavy and cumbersome. Everyone around me stared in disbelief and distrust. I buried myself into him and continued to cry.

Chapter 16

I heard Ethan turn off the lights in my room and draw the curtains closed. He hit shuffle on my iPod and a playlist of quiet, reflective music pushed me into calm. My head pounded and I couldn't open my eyes. I heard him settle himself into the easy chair near my bed. I felt him trying to calm me. I smelled his fear and a disappearing part of me reveled in it.

I was stuck in the battle that raged on inside my head. The darkest parts of me had grown stronger and fought against all that was good and right within me. The temptation to allow them to take over was powerful and consuming. I was more aware than ever of the choice I must make and more informed as to the difficulty I would have making it. It wasn't enough to want to stay Faithful. It wasn't enough to pretend it would all work out. I had to fight. I had to fight physically, emotionally, mentally, and spiritually. I had to fight for what was good. No wonder so many had joined Sebastian and his followers. It was ingrained in all of us to fall. To take the easy road. To fail.

I surprised myself when I finally decided to

speak. "I am tired of being stuck between two worlds. I don't know if I am strong enough to fight this. Everything crashes into me and I lose myself. I don't even know who I am anymore."

"You're a girl," Ethan said. "An angel, who was thrust into this without being informed. Without choice. You're Samantha English, a woman I've known my whole life. A woman I've protected my whole life. A woman I'm not allowed to love as I want to."

My throat dried at his words. "You love me?"

"Aww, Sam. You know I do. Jesse said he told you what I am. It's my duty to protect you, to keep you safe and I can't do that if I allow myself to get lost in what I feel for you. I always assumed it wouldn't be an issue since you and Lucas always seemed to have a 'thing'." He shifted in the chair as if he was trying to get comfortable. "The more it became apparent to me that, regardless of whatever feelings were out there, it would never happen, that you two would always be better as best friends, the more I allowed myself to test my emotions. And I can't protect you like that. Not like this."

Eerily, a haunting version of "Hallelujah" began to play and I shivered at the irony. Ethan was right. He and I couldn't be together, at least not now. Not until I cleared my head, fought the fight I'd been prepped for and saved Lucas. Maybe then. Only then.

"They must hate me."

"They don't hate you. They were caught off guard. We all knew your emotions were unstable. No one ever could've predicted what happened, though."

"I know you're right, Ethan. I feel it everywhere inside of me that you're right. I'm so sorry about all of this. I never meant to hurt anyone. I just had no control in the kitchen. And that's what they've been saying all along, huh? That I have no control. That's why they're so scared of me, wary of me. I should have listened better. You must be disappointed in me."

Crawling into the bed with me, he wrapped his arms around me, and whispered, "I could never be disappointed in you, Sam. Never. You are everything. You're stuck between worlds and we'll find a way for you to break free."

Black tears stained my pillow and I knew it would not end well.

"Okay, Ethan. Get me ready. But it better be soon. I can't guarantee how long I can keep this inside me. Whatever is going on has awakened something within me that wants to be unleashed. I want to be able to control it so I can point it in the right direction. I can't promise you anything other than that I will try. For you. I will try for you and for

243

Lucas and for my father."

"I know you will. Now get some sleep. We have a lot to think about."

His gentle kiss left me feeling sad. I could feel the pain he was in. I could feel the how torn he was over his feelings. For the first time, I concentrated on pulling the pain from him. I let it fill me up and consume me as the tension slowly left his beautiful face.

He drifted off while I mulled things over in my head. There was no way I would put anyone else in danger. If I couldn't control my outbursts, which were becoming more and more frequent and evermore dangerous, then I needed to figure out a way to do it all by myself. What if I had hurt Ethan? What if I had hurt someone else?

I needed to focus on finding Lucas. With every minute that passed, the more frightened I became. What if we couldn't find him? What if we couldn't save him? I couldn't live with myself if I caused pain to anyone else.

Samantha.

The knot in my stomach doubled in size at the sound of the voice that only I could hear. Not sure how to respond, I closed my eyes and let my father's voice seep in.

That's it Samantha. It's your turn now. It's

up to you to find Lucas. It's up to you to end this.

Dad? But how? How do I find him? How do I end this?

The necklace. Put it on and it will lead you to him. They have the box. You must find Lucas and get it back. You cannot defeat them without the box. Be careful. Once you're wearing the necklace, they will be able to find you, the Faithful and the Exiled. Until then, disappear. When you find them, put it on. If they take you, all will be lost.

Lost? What would happen if they took me? I didn't fully understand. It felt like even my father was speaking cryptically. Regardless, I became resolute in my decision. I knew what needed to be done.

I waited until I was sure Ethan was asleep and the house was quiet before I slipped out from under his arms. I turned to watch him sleep for a moment, brushing the hair out of his eyes and softly kissing him on the forehead. I quietly reached under the bed and pulled out my duffle. Time became a blur as I focused only on what I was about to do.

I dressed quietly, pulling on a pair of worn jeans and a black tank. I tugged on my favorite boots. Moving silently to the closet, I took out the leather jacket my dad gave me for my sixteenth birthday. He'd said it was my mom's. It was worn in and fit me like a glove. I smelled the leather and the faint scent of the life I'd left behind. The life I could never go back to. I opened the top drawer of my dresser and pulled out the emerald green pouch. I felt like I wasn't supposed to put it on yet so I stuffed it into the pocket of my jeans. I reached under the bed and retrieved my sword. The weight of it pulled at my heart. On the way out the door I lifted my iPod off its speaker dock and plugged in the ear buds. I took one last look at Ethan before I slid out the door, down the stairs and outside.

Chapter 17

There wasn't much time before daybreak and I needed to be careful. I knew the others were patrolling the area, probably still out looking for Lucas. Annoyance rose a bit before I tamped it down. Did I actually think, after today, they'd let me in on any of their plans to find Lucas? They probably didn't want anything to do with me and I didn't really blame them.

I shook off as much of the negativity as I could and focused on something Jesse had said earlier. I remembered my dad had mentioned it as well, about me being able to move about without detection. I had no idea how to do it though, so all I could think to do was concentrate on being invisible, the same way I would concentrate when I trained with Lucas and Ethan. I would concentrate on removing obstacles and they would disappear. Maybe all that focus training was for a reason.

I slipped behind a bush near the side of the house and glanced at my watch. One of them should be headed back soon; I knew they were trying to keep someone at the house at all times while the others searched and patrolled the area. I sat back on my heels and concentrated on being undetectable. It wasn't long before I was able to test out my theory.

Christian and Mara were walking up the driveway. I waited until they were close enough and stepped out from behind my hiding place. I was standing no more than twenty feet from them but they couldn't see me. I moved closer. Ten feet. They still had no idea I was there. It wasn't until I walked past them and brushed up against Mara that she looked around.

What was that? I must be imagining things. I could hear her thoughts.

A look of confused worry was etched on her otherwise beautiful face. They still couldn't see me. Satisfied, I smiled to myself. If I wasn't responsible for trying to save the world, I would've made one hell of a hide and seek partner. I quickened my step and headed for the cover of the woods.

Darkness blanketed everything and I didn't really know where to go other than to the cliff Jesse had brought me to. The one from my dreams. I relied on instinct, the one part of my training I'd always managed to get right. I stayed off the path as a precaution even though I was pretty sure no one could tell where I was. After all that had gone wrong, I didn't want to take any chances. A terrible feeling plagued me and I knew what happened next would be messy and destructive. But even so, I would do what I could to find Lucas, save him and annihilate anything, or anyone, that got in my way.

The night was quiet and gave me the time I needed to reflect on everything that'd happened. It felt like my soul was ripping into pieces. Nothing seemed to be working. If I really was supposed to choose between two worlds, I didn't understand why the choice was so difficult.

On one hand, the Faithful strived to maintain order and made up for the sins of others by preventing the Exiled from gaining any more control. They were fighting a losing battle because on the other hand, the Exiled flashed temptation, riches, fame and lust in the faces of those hungry for any opportunity to self satisfy. Part of me couldn't fathom why I couldn't commit. The obvious, right choice was for me to fight along side Ethan, Jesse and the others. The right choice was for me to meet Sebastian head on and avenge my father's death. But it was the whole avenging thing that cut me out of the Faithful loop. But, if I were a true Exiled, I didn't think I'd have been so hell bent on exacting revenge and destroying Sebastian.

There was also a part of me that grew stronger everyday and craved the ease with which the Exiled lived. They seemed to have no rules; they lived by nothing other than the simple motto of "do what feels good." And that was the difference, that they did what felt good, not *right*. At that point, I didn't even know why I bothered making a choice. It seemed, with my earlier aggression toward Scott and the others, the choice had been made for me. My only saving grace was Ethan. When I was out of control, he was the only one able to keep me grounded.

I sat against a tree to contemplate what all of it meant when the wind kicked up. Trees began to bow in submission and the clouds started to roll in. Something above me caught my eye. I was trying to figure out why it looked so familiar when the sound began. The hum. It was awful. I covered my ears and tried to block it out but it was louder than ever. The tree branches groaned and snapped violently. I looked up and saw the creature that had been haunting my dreams for months. It looked like a small winged man but its body was contorted oddly. It circled above me for a few minutes before diving through the trees where it disappeared. Within seconds I heard a piercing scream and sprinted toward the sound.

Just when I thought I'd lost my direction, I stumbled over something and fell flat on my face. Dead leaves swirled in every direction as I got up and dusted myself off, making it difficult to find what I'd tripped over.

It was Branna. "Branna! What happened?"

"That thing got me. It's one of the demons. It paralyzes you with a deafening noise then attacks. I think I got it though. Its wings are gone. It's over there." She jutted her dainty chin toward a cluster of trees.

Just behind them, huddled in pain, was the foulest creature I had ever laid my eyes on. Not quite as human as I imagined, it was the color of green mud with spindly wings that had fallen askew on the damp forest floor. Its arms and legs looked too long for its body and when I got closer, I noticed its sword. About two feet long, thin and deadly sharp, it looked more like a stinger. As I took a step closer, it moved suddenly and I jumped back, drawing my sword.

Its voice reminded me of gravel and fingernails on chalkboards. "You are Samantha."

Circling it, my anger intensified. "I am. And you are?"

"No matter. I know I will be dead in mere minutes. You, on the other hand, will die much more slowly and with greater pain than one could possibly imagine." The thing coughed and hacked. Its watery eyes were bulging and weak. The open wounds from where its wings had been cut off bubbled and oozed black blood. Its entire body was covered with scaly scabs and it emitted a fetid smell that burned my nose.

"What?"

"You will join Sebastian or you will die."

My blood boiled as sweat poured off me. "I won't join him." I lifted my sword.

"He is more to you than you know. He killed your father, you know. He will kill you too after he kills the boy, of course. The one who guards you. If you join him, he might be willing to spare at least *one* of you."

It was laughing when I plunged my sword into its chest. I stood over it, breath heavy and muscles shaking when it hit me that I had just killed. The realization wasn't as disturbing as I'd thought it would be and I turned away uncomfortable with my satisfaction.

I walked back to Branna and found her sitting up, injured but otherwise okay. She was startled by what I'd become. "Samantha, your eyes are so wide and black and shadows circle you".

I was still holding my sword and it dripped with black blood. "Branna. You need to go now."

She inched back while refusing to look me in the eye. "Samantha, stop. Ethan said this isn't you and I believe him. Let us help you."

Her courage was admirable considering I

could feel the fear pouring off of her. Amusement toyed at my mouth. I could do so much damage.

"I won't hurt you, Branna."

"Don't do this, Samantha. Wait for the others to come. We can help you."

Full of jealousy, I realized she had the ability to rely on others. "No. I have to do this on my own." Before I turned and ran into the cover of trees and darkness, I leaned down and placed my hands on her wounds. She began to heal the moment I touched her.

Clouds covered the moon throwing my world into a pitch of black. I couldn't keep the shadows from following me, entering me so I opened up and allowed them to take over. I couldn't keep the frustration, anger or confusion at bay and they threatened to swallow me whole.

Once, a long time ago now it seemed, I was a normal teenaged girl. There was nothing spectacular about me. Now, nothing about me was normal. I'd become hollow, a mere shell for the shadows to fill as they pleased.

A half hour later, I stopped suddenly when I heard footsteps off to my left. They were getting closer. Just through the brush I could see Scott and Noah. *Great.* Why did it have to be the two who hated me the most? They stopped to take a break, Scott standing, scanning the area, while Noah was sitting, his back up against a tree. I concentrated so they won't sense me.

"I don't trust her."

"I don't trust her either but my dad says we should give her space. He says she's the only thing we have left to win this fight."

They were talking about me and my fingers started to itch. I took a few steps closer to hear them better.

"If it were up to me, I would've killed her the moment I stepped into the house. Can't you feel the darkness that rolls off her? She's evil. She's one of them."

I stepped closer as my irritation teetered on anger.

"I know. I can feel it. But with it, intertwined is the purest light I've ever come across. I don't know what to do with her. I just have to trust my dad."

"No offense, Scott, but your dad is a bit too trusting for my taste. The only reason I'm here is because Cal asked me to join him and because of James."

James? My dad, James? For a second, my vision cleared and something twitched in my heart.

"I know." Scott sighed. "I don't know. With this, I guess I'll just do as I'm told."

Noah suddenly stood at attention and cocked

his ear into the night.

He whispered, "Scott. Did you hear that?"

"I did." Scott pulled his sword from its sheath on his back.

At first I thought they'd recognized me but their eyes were focused in the opposite direction. They took a few steps off the path and I heard a great crash that sounded like smashing rocks. It was hard to see but I heard what sounded like a scuffle. Someone yelled out and my instincts took over. I dropped my duffle and pulled out my sword. I now knew what it was like to use it even if the thought made me squeamish.

I crept toward the noises. Noah was battling with some winged creature, similar to the one I killed earlier. They were yelling things at each other, both with wings fully extended. I'd never seen anyone able to throw another with such strength and force; it was mesmerizing. I heard something a few yards away and turned my head to see what it was.

"You won't win. Sebastian is too strong," growled a winged shadow as Scott nailed it with his sword.

"No matter. At least I'll be able to rid the world of you," Scott yelled back as he hit the leg of the shadow with such force that it lost its balance and stumbled.

The two of them were locked in a dance to the death. Both were deft with their respective swords. Scott's was a fiery red that reminded me of flames and the other carried a heavy stone-gray sword. The noises emanating from them when they clashed were ear splitting. Just when it seemed Scott had the upper hand, the shadow swung his sword from behind and sliced off Scott's wings. A terrible groan of pain escaped Scott's lips before he fell to the ground, bloody. The shadow walked over and kicked Scott onto his back. My hand flew to my mouth. I ran towards him but I knew it would be too late.

The dark shadow stood over him with his sword pointed at Scott's chest. Before I could do anything, it pushed the sword into Scott's heart. I heard Scott murmur a 'screw you' before the light dimmed from his eyes. I was so astonished I was struck dumb. I didn't even scream out but my anger was building up again. The familiar twist in my stomach, haze in my eyes and nerve-piercing vibration reared its ugly head. This time, however, my intent was on slaughtering the thing that killed Scott.

In a rage I exposed myself to the shadow and it howled in delight. With my sword drawn, I suddenly felt weak but I knew I couldn't think that way. I had to let it know I was strong and ready for a fight. I wouldn't be able to fight if I didn't allow the darkness in.

"So, Samantha. The one we've been waiting for. Sebastian will be so happy to see you."

Its laugh was sickening and a wave of nausea threatened to overwhelm me. Still, my resolve to destroy it continued to build and I struck first. Surprised at my first move, it still easily blocked my blows. It was toying with me. "You're gonna have to do better than that, my dear. Haven't those boys taught you anything?"

The mere mention of Lucas and Ethan fueled my need for destruction and I dove into myself, pulled forward all the training I'd been through and redoubled my efforts. I swung the sword from overhead and sliced its arm open. Black blood bubbled from the wound and it was momentarily stunned. I used surprise to my advantage and spun around for a second blow, this time to the other arm. It squealed in pain as its arm fell to the ground, leaving only a bloody stump still attached to its body.

"You will pay. I will see to it." The shadow came at me with such ferocity I could barely fight back. It wasn't until Noah attacked it from behind that I was able to do any damage.

The thing turned around to see what hit it and I used the opportunity to hack its scaly black wings off. What came out of its mouth was so piercing, my ears rang and I was deaf for a moment. I watched as Noah drove his sword into its heart and swiftly pulled it out. The last words out of the thing's mouth were, "You're all dead."

Scratched and bloody, Noah looked at me. His wings were damaged and he was having trouble standing up straight. He wasn't as surprised by the look of me as Branna was. He must've expected me to look like that and though distrust was still evident, he surprised me with a 'thank you'. "Have you seen Scott?"

I turned and walked towards Scott's motionless body. I placed my hand gently over his eyes and closed them.

"Noah, he's dead. I watched that thing cut off his wings and then drive its sword into his chest. It caught him by surprise. I really thought he had it."

Noah stared at Scott's lifeless body lying on the ground with bluish-purple wings strewn about like afterthoughts. Noah walked over, picked up Scott's body and asked me to lay the wings over him, like a blanket. I did so and couldn't help but notice how light the wings felt in my hands, like there was no weight to them at all.

"I must bring him back to his father and get the others. You'd do well to stay put. They will kill you, Samantha, even if you join them. Sebastian won't let you live. You are too powerful for him to allow you to remain alive. And, regardless of my earlier and personal distrust of you, I want to thank you for taking care of the one who did this to Scott."

I reached out and ran my fingers down Noah's injured wings.

"It's time for you to go now. As for them killing me, that still remains to be seen. You do what you have to but don't think I will stay here. I have to face him. I have to find Lucas. I need to do this. If the others come, they can help find Lucas. Sebastian is for me to deal with."

For the first time he looked at me like he understood and nodded curtly. With Scott's body, he disappeared into the woods. I regained my focus to hide myself and turned back in the direction of my destination.

Chapter 18

Samannnnnnthaaaa…Where are you, silly girl?

I froze in my tracks. Sebastian. I heard some of the others talking about how he liked to taunt his prey. I guessed I was no exception. My nerves danced and I instinctively shut my eyes to keep the darkness at bay before I realized the darkness was exactly what would help me as it had moments before. I needed to concentrate. He wouldn't find me if I concentrated.

Samannnnnnthaaaa…Are you hiding from me? I have your precious Lucas here. He's waiting for you. Better hurry. He hasn't got much time.

I heard a deep moan of pain. Lucas! *Sonofabitch!* My head was screaming and I broke into a run, all the while doing all I could to remain hidden. I broke through into the clearing where Jesse and I had our discussion only hours before. The memory slowed me for a moment before I heard the moan again. Was it in my head? Was it close? It sounded like it was everywhere and nowhere. I scanned my surroundings. Nothing. I had to get to the cliff. That was where Jesse said 'it' was to happen. I just hoped 'it' involved me saving Lucas and destroying Sebastian.

I raced to the other side and found myself in the thickest part of the woods. I stopped just before I hit the opening that led to the cliff. I crouched low behind a tree and listened. I was fidgety and my eyes were constantly moving. I shifted my position several times but nothing shook out the restless excitability. I heard murmured voices, but I had no idea who they belonged to but they were talking about me. One of them had to be Sebastian and he sounded angry.

"You said she would come."

"She'll come. I promise. There's no way she won't." The second voice was so low and gravelly I could barely make out what he was saying.

"She better or you will pay for it."

"Patience, Sebastian."

My ears perked up. The voice, below the gravel, was familiar and I searched my memories for who it could've belonged to.

"Don't speak to me of patience. You know I have none."

Sebastian's tone was sharp and dangerous. As he spoke, thunder boomed like an exclamation point. "This one won't be too difficult. She teeters between both worlds. I fear it may be too easy to convince her."

"You might be right, Sebastian. She's so confused, she doesn't know which way is up. I've never met anyone so conflicted. The blood of the Faithful and the Exiled both course through her veins. It's a wonder she hasn't gone insane."

Sebastian spoke in a whisper that floated into nothing. "Her existence has always been that of mere myth. It was foretold once, long ago, there would be an angel that walked both worlds, one that would follow the path of both light and dark. One that embodies both hopes and despairs equally. She's dangerous and she needs to be destroyed."

"I'll do it myself if I have to." Who *was* that? I knew that voice.

"I know you will. We must get The Heart of Hope from her first."

"She'll be wearing it when she comes."

"How can you be sure?"

"She thinks we're friends and she'll do what she thinks she should to rescue me."

No. Realization dawned and tears immediately stung my eyes, threatening to spill over. *What the hell?* I felt like I'd just had the wind knocked out of me. I doubled over and forced down the bile that had risen into my throat. *It couldn't be!*

I shook my head to rid myself of the terrible things I'd just heard. Lucas hadn't been attacked? He

263

hadn't been kidnapped? Had he really joined them? I couldn't process the fact that he was now an Exiled.

Chapter 19

Oily black tears stung my eyes and stained my cheeks. Confusion swirled around me and I felt dizzy with grief and the refusal to believe Lucas couldn't still be saved... *But how? When?* I didn't understand. *Lucas? Not possible.* Lucas was my best friend, how could I have not known. A wave of sadness tightened its fist around my heart. I shuffled through my brain looking for a clue I might have missed, any tiny nuance that should have alerted me to this. There was nothing. I wanted to scream out but instead I shoved my fist in my mouth to keep silent.

Lucas became the face of betrayal, of hate. There he was, arm in arm with the bastard that killed my father. There would be no forgiveness. The wound went too deep. *Lucas is going to find himself facing a greater wrath than Sebastian*, I promised as my thinking shifted from rescue to destruction.

Does Ethan know? I wondered. *Oh my God.* Was Ethan one of them too? All that talk about guardian angels, could it be that he was an Exiled too? The thought drove a stake of distrust into my soul. I couldn't let it drive me over the edge, not just yet anyway. I had to hear more. I moved closer to the edge of the thicket.

"What about your brother?" Sebastian inquired calmly.

"What about him?" Lucas snaked back.

"Will he be joining us, too?

"No."

"No?"

"No. Ethan won't be joining us. He's too enamored with the Faithful and with *her* to have any part of this."

I felt like I was going crazy. Whispers invaded my space, paranoia shimmied up my spine and raw, naked loathing filled me. I was almost ready to confront them. I needed to allow it all to consume me. I needed to become the darkness I'd been trained to run from. I needed to extinguish that small part of me that road blocked the shadows.

"Maybe we can convince him."

Lucas turned to face Sebastian, his face mangled by hate. "No. He doesn't belong here. He'd rather die than join us. I don't want him here."

"Are you afraid he might join us? That he might figure out who I am and run back with open arms? That once he does, I might discard you?" Sebastian cackled with menace.

Lucas sounded defeated. The blustery tone he

spewed a moment ago was now overpowered by Sebastian's sarcasm. "If that is what you want. But he won't be easy to turn. He's her guardian."

"And her?"

"Her who? Samantha? She's just a silly little girl who has something we need. She'll be of no use to us after we get the pendant."

"Is *that* all she is to you, Lucas? A *Silly. Little. Girl.*"

As he spoke those last taunting words, Sebastian turned to face the woods and I saw him fully for the first time. He'd been an idea, a whispered-about entity, a shadow. And now I could see him fully. I was not ready for what I saw. Sebastian was not at all the ugly, twisted evil I envisioned. Instead, his beauty was undeniable. His caramel colored skin, short dark brown hair and green eyes were captivating. He was tall and slim but obviously strong. His wings were large and full, the color of oil on asphalt, shifting between iridescent colors with each movement. He was wearing leather pants, heavy boots and no shirt. Even the way he stood commanded attention and loyalty while instilling fear and despair. I was quite certain the thought of betrayal by any one of his subjects would've been met with swift and brutal punishment. He was the most terrifyingly beautiful creature I'd ever seen. I'd never been more frightened in my life.

"That is all she is. All she ever was. All she ever will be."

You bastard, I thought to myself. I couldn't run from the fact that he'd been my best friend, basically my brother, for the past seventeen years. I forced the thought from my mind and focused on how I was going to kill him.

"But I've kept watch, Lucas. I've seen the way you wanted her to look at you. The way you wanted her to think about you when she is all alone in her bedroom. The way you imagined her eyes would close when she thought of you..."

"Enough, Sebastian!"

Sebastian's laugh was slow and deep. "What's the matter? I thought she was just a silly little girl. Shall I, then, refrain from discussing her interlude with Ethan? Shall I refrain from reminding you how she let him touch her? How she touched him?"

Lucas stiffened and turned to face him.

Sebastian clapped like a child who'd found his Christmas presents early. "Oh! You didn't know? How terribly delightful."

Lucas charged at Sebastian and barreled into him like a linebacker. Still laughing, Sebastian lazily tossed Lucas off of him like a rag doll. He calmly walked over and lifted Lucas by his neck so his feet no longer touched the ground. Sebastian's wings beat once and they were both suspended five feet above the rocky earth. The sun quietly began to creep over the horizon and Sebastian's face took on an eerie glow.

His voice boomed in time with the sudden sound of thunder and the wind took on the strength of a tornado. "You listen to me, boy. I may have taken you under my wing. I may have promised you would rule as my right hand if you delivered the girl but if she doesn't show, you will meet the same fate as her father! Please have no illusions that you actually mean anything. There are dozens more who would relish the opportunity I have given you."

He threw Lucas off the edge of the cliff to the wailing ocean below. Lucas caught himself and flew upward meeting Sebastian, toe to suspended toe. "I told you. She will come. You have my word."

"Your word is no good until promises are delivered."

It was all too much. I reached into my pocket and took out the pouch. It was time. I placed my sword next to me as I opened the pouch and poured the necklace into the palm of my hand. I could feel the rage in my belly. I knew my eyes had completely darkened to orbs of coal black hate. Deception fueled me now. Heartless betrayal and duplicitous

269

malevolence forced themselves into focus. I slipped the necklace over my head and picked up my sword.

Sebastian's head immediately snapped in my direction. A seedy grin stretched across his now twisted face. "Ah, she's here," he whispered. His eyes scanned our surroundings and he pinpointed my location. He clasped his hands together. "Come out, Samantha. Lucas, look who has decided to join us. I see you've worn the necklace as he said you would."

I squared my shoulders to step out into the clearing when someone grabbed my hand. I pulled back and raised my sword as I turned to see who held me.

Ethan. "Samantha, no. He's going to kill you."

"How did you…?"

"Noah brought Scott back to the house. I was leaving the house to look for you. He told me where you might be headed. Then you put on the necklace and I could finally sense you."

"You need to go."

"No, Sam. Let's get Lucas and get out of here. The others are on the way. Let them deal with Sebastian."

He no longer had trouble looking at me when I was like this. Shadows poured out of me, my eyes protruded black and my skin heated up with fury. His worry and concern were uninvited guests that I had no patience for. My voice firm, I warned him. "Lucas isn't going anywhere, Ethan."

"What? Why?"

"Lucas is one of them, Ethan."

"What? What are you talking about?"

"*Samannnnnnthaaaa*," Sebastian taunted.

"Your brother is an Exiled."

"Come out, come out wherever you are." Sebastian's sing song had taken on the sound of screechy nails.

"No. Sam, you don't know what…"

"She doesn't know what, Ethan?"

Lucas was standing behind us, wings completely outstretched with intimidation. Ethan turned; confusion and uncertainty plagued his face. It wasn't until Lucas grabbed him by the neck and threw him into the opening did realization dawn on him. I lifted my sword in retaliation but it was pulled from my hands by Sebastian's will.

"Walk," Lucas looked at me with hate and I refused to flinch.

I turned from him and walked defiantly into the open. Exiled followers littered the rocky clearing. Some looked like the nasty scaly creatures I'd dealt with earlier, others looked like regular people and still others took on the beauty and grace of every other angel.

Each set of wings were different colors, textures, shapes and sizes, and they suddenly reminded me of fingerprints. Sebastian's nasty grin grew wider and his face, no longer handsome, had taken on a demonic undertone. His cheekbones sharpened and his eyes widened to black spheres. All the darkness inside me swirled with loyalty and I was drawn to him. Fighting to remain in control of deception, I walked slowly and deliberately toward him. My sword was at his feet and I made no move to retrieve it. Instead I stood tall in front of him.

"How wonderful to finally meet you!" He was giddy with sarcasm. As his long fingers traced the outline of my face, I closed my eyes. "Look at me!"

I slowly opened them and locked his gaze in defiance.

"Good girl."

I heard Ethan struggling to get up behind me but I made no move to turn in his direction. I stood tense and waited for what was to come. As long as I didn't fight, I knew they wouldn't hurt Ethan. It was a feeling I couldn't explain but it was all I had to rely on.

"Damien," Sebastian called to one of his minions, snapping his long fingers. "Retrieve the box."

Damien's scarred face twisted in delight

before he bowed in submission. "As you wish." Damien was tall and gangly with greasy hair and he was dressed in an old-fashioned, tattered suit, like he'd stepped into the present from the 1950's. His fingernails were long and yellow and the smell that came from him was so putrid, I struggled to breathe. In a second the Exiled was airborne and disappeared into the horizon.

All was silent until I heard the drawing of swords and a familiar voice. "Let them go, Sebastian."

Jesse. Only when I heard his voice did I look away from Sebastian. They were all there. Christian and Mara, Noah, Cal and Branna, all with swords drawn, wings opened and ready for battle.

"Look, we have an audience. How wonderful." The Exiled giggled at Sebastian's words as they, too, drew their swords.

"Samantha, give me the necklace."

"No," I responded forcefully.

"Give me the necklace. Please."

"Are you deaf? I said no."

The look in his eye was deadly but the angrier he got, the more his frustration swelled, the stronger I felt. I was beginning to understand. I didn't have to give up the darkness to join the Faithful. They needed shadows to have any chance of defeating Sebastian and his followers. The small revelation glowed inside me while encouraging me to fade to black.

"Sebastian, let her go."

"Now, now, Jesse. Do you honestly think I am going to give up the one thing that will guarantee me a victory? With her at my side, I can finally be rid of all of you *Faithful* followers."

Sebastian walked slowly behind me and whispered in my ear. "What are you fighting for anyway, Samantha? Redemption? Forgiveness? *His* favor? He won't give it, you know. As far as He is concerned, you're all as Fallen as I am. I just choose to embrace the freedom afforded me by His distaste."

Jesse's voice grew louder. "You won't win, Sebastian. It's a losing battle. Let her go."

"I think not." As he completed his walk around, Sebastian turned back to face me. He cocked his head slightly to the side and asked, "You will not give me what I ask for?"

"No."

"Very well."

With a small gesture, he commanded another Exiled to step forward all the while keeping his eyes fixed on mine. "Kill him." The smirk on his face dared me to save Jesse. I heard the two fighting behind me but I refused to break eye contact to watch. Swords clashed, words taunted and torrential rain fell from the sky.

Sebastian continued to watch my eyes. He seemed to be waiting for me to break and no doubt, he was betting on it. I was standing toe to toe with Evil Incarnate and I didn't want to give in, but I couldn't sit there and listen to Jesse die. I could tell he was getting tired and it was only a matter of time before he met his fate. I looked to Ethan and saw he was unconscious, held up like a rag doll by his abomination of a brother.

"Wait! Stop!"

Sebastian, eyes still focused on mine, smiled wickedly. He held up a hand and the fighting ceased. "Yes?"

"I'll do what you want. Just let everyone else go."

He rubbed his chin thoughtfully, toying with me. "Let them go. Let them go? And you'll give me the pendant?"

"I will. Just take me from here and I will give it to you. I want to leave here so I know you won't hurt them. Leave them be and I will go with you and give you what you want."

Our faces were inches apart and he was searching me for deception as I searched him for the same. Satisfied he could find none, he snapped his fingers and all the Exiled took to the skies and the swords fell from the hands of the Faithful. Christian, Mara, Branna, Cal, Noah and Jesse focused on me and I felt myself heat up with light.

Lucas lifted off the ground with Ethan in tow.

"Wait! I said leave them be! That means Ethan, too. He stays."

"Don't you know the rules of negotiation? He is leverage, my dear. How am I to be sure you will do as I say?" Sebastian's laugh was filled with amusement.

Contempt tried to force its way out of me but I remained silent as I began to float off the ground.

"Oh. One more thing," Sebastian whispered in my ear. "If you try to betray me, this is what will happen to Ethan and everyone you have ever met."

He forced my face downward where I could see Jesse standing, looking up at us. Suddenly, two winged creatures appeared out of nowhere and ambushed Jesse. Within moments his wings were shredded and a sword pierced his heart. It was so fast no one, Jesse or the other Faithful, had time to react. I didn't even have time to flinch before I was whisked away. Sadness, once again, filled me.

Chapter 20

I was alone, chained to the floor. I didn't know where I was, only that it was dark and damp and furtive whispers echoed from everywhere. A desperate and futile hope plagued me. Hope that my father would reach out from the dead to help me. I felt guilty for allowing Sebastian to take me but what other choice did I have? I couldn't let him kill the others.

An image of Jesse fired in my mind. Anger surged through me and the walls of my prison shook and crumbled. "Sebastian! Sebastian! Show yourself!" I screamed his name over and over to no avail. He didn't come. My voice, hoarse from yelling, burned with hatred. I looked around for something, anything I could use to break free. The room was empty. There were no windows, no furniture, and I was the only occupant.

I thought of Lucas, how his betrayal had filled my heart with vengeance.

I thought of my father, how his passing had left me broken hearted and ill prepared for this fight.

I thought of Ethan, how his heart had been my one and only tether to the Faithful. I needed to get to him, to save him. But I didn't know how. The tables had been turned, it seemed and I now needed to save the one that guarded me.

I thought of Jesse and Scott, a father and son, who gave their lives for what they believed in.

I thought of the others, the remaining Faithful and hoped I could do what was needed to make up for this. This colossal mess that centered on me.

I thought of humanity and prayed that there was hope enough left in the world to ease them out of all this evil when everything was said and done.

I closed my eyes and tried to control the hatred inside me. I needed to funnel it in the direction it needed to go. But I couldn't stop it from consuming me, overwhelming me. In addition to everything I'd learned, darkness was the real gift I'd been left with. I needed to own it in order to use it to defeat Sebastian. Light hadn't worked so it was time I used darkness and beat him at his own game but it was too strong, too undisciplined and it fought to break free. I knew if I allow it to escape, my father's warning would come true.

All would be lost.

I had no idea how long I'd been chained there. Days turned into nights. Nights turned into days and still I was left there, confined to that space, manacled to the floor. I'd had no company other than the mangled thoughts that screamed through my head. I'd had plenty of time to think. To *really* think, and the darkness was about to swallow me whole.

Apple cores littered the floor; the one thing Sebastian had allowed me. After about the fifth Macintosh I realized the irony of the fruit. It was the apple, after all that signaled the end of ignorance and opened the eyes of man to despair and temptation. A plan set in motion by Sebastian and carried out by Lucifer, the original fallen angel.

Sebastian liked to play his little games.

With nothing to do, no one to talk to, my mind wandered to Ethan. I didn't know where he was and the hope that I would find him was fading quickly. I was sure they had killed him. So much time had passed and I wasn't sure he was alive for me to save.

My hands reached to my neck. I still had the necklace. It was still hanging around my neck, waiting to be snatched and destroyed. Why it hadn't been done already, was beyond me.

After what seemed like an eternity, I heard muffled footsteps that grew louder with each step. The door creaked open and a sliver of light peaked through the opening, momentarily blinding me. The door clicked closed. When the halos left my sight, I was face to face with Lucas.

The temporary calm that had settled over me

since I'd been there evaporated and everything hateful inside me rose to the surface. I screamed and kicked at my shackles. My teeth chipped away as I tried to bite my way through the chains and still he sat there, calm and amused.

"You might want to calm down, Samantha."

"Screw you," I spat back.

"Actually, it looks like you're the one who's screwed."

"You son of a bitch! How could you? You were my best friend! For seventeen years we've been joined at the hip. You lived in my house! My father took you in when your dad died and this is how you repay him? By teaming up with the one who killed him? You're a backstabber! A liar!"

He spewed venom. "Best friends, huh? Is that what you think? Maybe once upon a time. But when we got older, when my father died, while you were following me around like a damned puppy dog, waiting for me to throw any scrap of romantic interest your way, I was doing as I was told. I began looking for the box, looking for the pendant. I couldn't very well do that if we were enemies, now could I?" His words stung worse than I could've ever imagined.

A monster roared inside me, clawing away what was left of my soul, trying to get out. I fought and pulled against the chains, my wrists shredding into a bloody mess.

"What feelings are you talking about? What romantic interest? You were my friend. There was no romantic anything. Sebastian is playing with you."

"Liar!"

"What is wrong with you? This isn't the Lucas I know. This isn't the Lucas I grew up with. Open your eyes, Lucas! Don't you see? Sebastian is controlling you. He must be because *my* Lucas would never do this. *My* Lucas was kind and compassionate. *My* Lucas would never allow this to continue! Why? Why the charade? Why all the deception? Have you been lying all this time?"

"You are so stupid. *Your* Lucas? I was never *your* Lucas. None of it was real, Samantha. Get that through your thick skull! It. Wasn't. Real. If I wanted to act on the feelings you had, I could have. Easily. Unfortunately, the mere thought of it makes me ill. You make me ill, but I had to get close to you in order to get close to your father. When my father died, I knew my calling was to follow Sebastian. Do you think James would divulge anything to just anyone? No. I had to gain his trust. Unfortunately, he wouldn't tell me what I needed to know." Lucas kicked an apple core at me and whispered, "He did, however, tell me where he would be the night he was killed. And I may have just happened to let that slip to

281

Sebastian."

I hated him. I hated him with every fiber of my being. I hated him with purpose. With every utterance that poured out of his mouth, with every roll of his eyes, with every egotistical smirk that I once thought endearing, I hated him more. I wanted him to feel the pain I felt. I wanted him to meet the fate he sealed for my father.

He stood and started walking to the door. Pausing, he turned and looked me square in the eye. "You know, Sam, had you any ounce of conviction or purpose, you know you wouldn't be here right now. You had all the power and means to destroy Sebastian but with all your wishy-washy indecision, you missed the perfect opportunity. But you're stupid. And now he's going to kill you."

"What about Ethan?" I yelled. "He's your brother! Think of him! Have you allowed Sebastian to dispose of him too? How could you just so callously throw us all away? We were family!"

He stiffened with his hand on the doorknob and I thought he was going to turn back and attack. Black tears streamed down my face and pooled on the concrete floor. Everything around me swayed and hummed.

When he spoke, his voice was cold and distant. "I don't have a brother, Sam. I never did."

Chapter 21

A scaly hand yanked me by my hair and shook me awake. Two creatures unlocked the chains, peeling off the shackles and reopening the wounds underneath. Roughly, they pulled me to my feet and shuffled me out the door. Physically, I was weak. Mentally, I'd never been sharper, despite being isolated in a dark room. It was like the darkness had been fine-tuning my awareness, preparing me for whatever came next.

With swords at my back, I was told to walk. The hallway was dimly lit, but my eyes still had trouble adjusting to the dismal light. Hands clasped tightly in front of me, I walked slowly. My mind raced, waiting for any opportunity to strike out at my guards. Behind me, I could hear their excited whispers of glee. They thought Sebastian had won. They thought he was going to rule the world.

They thought wrong. This wasn't over yet.

"Where are you taking me?" I asked, feigning desperation.

"Shut up!" One of them knocked me to the ground and my face bounced off the concrete floor.

Something wet dripped onto my lips and it tasted metallic. I wiped my arm across my face. Blood was flowing from my nose. Something inside me smiled wickedly. The pain was just the jolt I needed, and my resolve and my physical strength came roaring back.

The other one kicked me. "Get up! Move!"

Head down, I answered meekly. "I can't. I need help."

Each of my captors grabbed one of my arms and pulled me to my feet. I stumbled and they curse at me as they forced me upright. A wry smile played at my mouth; time to put all that training to work. I picked my head up, squared my shoulders and held my hands together in front of me. I swung my arms around and caught the first Exiled off guard. He dropped his sword and I willed it to fly into my hand. I slashed the other one across the chest with a force that threw him backward. Spinning around, I pulled the first to his feet and immediately hacked off his wings. My left hand outstretched, I held the other one at bay and aimed the sword at the first Exiled's chest. He looked at me with hatred and defiance. In his eyes I saw nothing but the dark reflection of myself. I unflinchingly pushed the sword into him. I turned to the second Exiled and, with a flick of my palm he crashed into the wall and slumped to the ground.

I slowly stepped over to him and lifted him up

by his chin. "Where is Ethan?"

He laughed and I deftly sliced off one of his wings. He screamed like a wounded animal.

"Let's try this again. Where is Ethan?"

"Ethan is no longer."

"Is he dead?"

His laugh became maniacal as he said, "He may as well be."

I quickly sliced off his other wing and whispered, "Where is he?"

"He is with Sebastian. You will not be allowed to take him back. He is no longer your guardian."

"Maybe not," I said and plunged the sword into him with every last ounce of strength inside me. "But I am his."

He smiled at me. "You are darker than all of us," he said, his laughter fading into silence.

***

It took me a moment before I could regain my bearings. I was still not entirely comfortable with my transformation. Buried deep down was the knowledge that I needed to remain on the side of the Faithful. However, much closer to the surface was the fear I would not be able to escape the hold of the Exiled. The darkness that had permeated my being played tricks on me. I saw a dark future for myself; I saw the anger and rage that consumed me. I longed for my father, for his advice and knowledge and I feared he wouldn't be able to reach me. Not while I was submerged in shadows. But I couldn't allow the thought to distract me from my goal. I needed to find Ethan, destroy Lucas and get rid of Sebastian once and for all.

The sword in my hand felt heavier than mine but since I had no idea what Lucas had done with it; this one would have to do. A few feet down the hall the stone passageway made a sharp left that led to a set of steep, narrow stairs. I took them two at a time. At the top was two passages, one ahead and one to the right. I knew one would lead me to Sebastian. The fact that I didn't know which suddenly put me on edge.

I'd tried to remain clear on my objective, drilling it into my brain the past few days and now that I was out of my chains and ready for confrontation, the simple matter of navigation threw me for a loop. I needed to get a handle on this. My eyes flicked from corridor to corridor until I was dizzy. My breathing got heavy and I crouched, head leaning on the sword, trying to clear my head. *What was happening to me?*

Samantha. I am here.

Dad? I'd been so sure he couldn't reach me here. I didn't think he could while I was so dark.

Which way do I go? Dad, help me.

Samantha. I am so sorry. I wish I could be there, to help guide you.

You can! Just tell me what I need to do.

I cannot.

Why? Dad, please!

This is your destiny. Your choices determine the course.

But I don't know which way. I need to save Ethan!

Think Samantha. Think about Ethan. Focus on him and you will find him. You can find him if you clear your head. Sebastian expects Ethan to return to him and ask for forgiveness.

What do you mean 'return to him'? Why would Ethan need to ask Sebastian for forgiveness?

You know the answer.

I was so sick of the damned riddles! *I don't know the answer and I don't know what is happening to me, dad.*

Your transformation is almost complete. You will be the one who walks between both dark and light.

Wasn't that the same thing Sebastian had said? *I need your help finding Lucas. He betrayed me.*

I need your help when I confront him. I can't do this on my own.

I cannot because it is revenge you seek. The Faithful do not follow paths forged from vengeance. You must do this not out of hate but of love.

Was he abandoning me? I shook my head in frustration. He wasn't allowed do this to me. Everyone I loved was gone. He couldn't be gone, too. *I have to do this! I have to make them pay for what they did to you, for what they are probably doing to Ethan. How can you not help your own daughter?*

It hurts me to be unable to help you with this. You have to look beyond the hate and find the real reason for your anger. Anger fueled by love will not condemn you. Anger in spite of love makes you no better than those you seek to destroy. Everything you need is inside you. Trust yourself and you will find what you seek.

What do you mean? What am I looking for?

He didn't answer. He was gone and I was no closer to the answers I needed. How the hell was I supposed to do this alone? I was not strong enough. I was not ready. I held the pendant in my palm and stared at it like it was going to give me something. I mourned the loss of my father. I mourned Lucas' betrayal. I mourned a beginning that was cut short. Ethan. What could've been something enlightening

288

was cut short by Lucas' betrayal, Sebastian's manipulations.

A single inky tear fell on the Heart and it began to shine. Images rose from it like photographs. I saw my father, proud and happy. Though born into darkness, he remained Faithful to the final end. His loyalty to the Faithful was to be celebrated. He gave his life for all of ours. Snapshots of Lucas and the betrayal that showed through his eyes all along stung me. Betrayal I was never ready for. Betrayal I could never forgive. Other pictures of our friendship flashed quickly. That was what I was really mourning, the loss of my best friend, of my family. The betrayal was what fueled me but the love I had held me up.

A final image spun into sight. Ethan stood behind me on my right side, radiating bright white light. Spread out beside him were silver wings. I thought it odd considering Ethan didn't have wings but, sure enough, he had them in this image. His eyes were focused on me and they were full of love. My father was the love that would always follow me. Lucas was the love that broke me and Ethan was the love that would heal me, put me back together and help me stay balanced. He would never let me fall into the depths of the Exiled.

The revelation hit me like bricks. Tons of them. I now knew which way to go.

I stood, prepared to meet my fate and ran toward where I knew they were keeping Ethan. With every step, the pendant glowed brighter. I knew I was close. Two more Exiled met me in the narrow tunnel. I made quick work of dispatching them and moved on. Murmured voices grew louder with every stride. At the end of the tunnel, I came to a heavy wooden door.

It was identical to the door I'd passed through everyday for the last six months. The door of the cabin. They were the same. And they had the same markings and wood as the box. The carvings swirled and their whispers floated out to me, sounding like gibberish. My ears started to ring and I swiped at my clothes, feeling something crawling on me, which I frantically tried to get rid of. The sounds and movements ceased the moment I put my hand on the door and pushed it open.

The room was large, reminding me of a church. Against the back wall was an altar of sorts. Above me, light streamed through dingy stained glass windows, giving the room a reddish glow. Despite the filthy windows, the lights were much brighter in there than the hallway and again I had to allow my eyes to adjust. Standing in the middle of the room, smiling at me with arms wide open was Sebastian. Lucas was off to the left with a look of horror on his face. At his feet was a crumpled and unconscious Ethan.

I swiftly took in the surroundings then immediately threw my palm at Lucas and hurled him against the wall. When he hit the floor, I pulled him to me and dropped him like a doll at my feet.

"Samantha, what a delight! We were just speaking of you." Sebastian's handsome face faded back and forth between beauty and monster.

"I'm here now. Let Ethan go."

"We've gone over this, silly girl. Give me the pendant and I will let one of you live."

"Why didn't you just take it? You had me locked up long enough."

"It seems there was a snag. You see, I did try to remove it from your neck but," he held up his blistered hands, "as long as you are alive, it is not for me to take. You must give it to me. Something I, of course, should have foreseen but lesson learned."

"Why didn't you just kill me then?"

He lifted his chin and smiled at me. "Well, I would have but you are so…interesting. Your existence has been whispered about for so long, we all thought you were a myth. I thought I would get to know you first, make you see reason. With you at my side, there is nothing we cannot accomplish."

"Wanna be friends now, Sebastian?"

"Friends, partners, enemies. It's all the same
291

to me. There is also the little fact that I can't figure out how to actually kill you. Of course, I will find out the why's and how's and then remedy the situation. But, for now, we are at an impasse of sorts. Unless, of course, you agree to join me." He smiled charmingly, bowing, just a little towards me as if he were some kind of gentleman.

I looked at Ethan, limp on the floor. "Will you let him go?"

Sebastian threw his hands in the air in mock exasperation. "What *is* it with you? What on earth do you have to gain from saving him? If it's pleasure you want, then pleasure I have to give. Let me show you what you have to gain from joining me."

The sheer perversion of his words made my stomach turn. "I love him. Let him go and I will give you the Heart of Hope."

"Love him? What do you know of love? You *are*, indeed, a silly girl. You love Lucas. You love Ethan. You cannot make up your mind, can you? I can see into that black hole you call a heart and I see nothing but hatred and revenge. You can't know love if you draw your strength from hate. I am surprised *daddy* didn't tell you that. I mean, really, why save *this* one? Because he's your guardian angel? They are a dime a dozen. At least one a day pledges his allegiance to me. Or better yet, join me and you won't need an angel to keep you safe."

I hated the egotistical bragging that dripped from his words.

"I won't join you, Sebastian. You know that. And if all you see inside me is hate, then why did you flinch when I mentioned love? You know I have it in me. You know I walk the thin line between the Exiled and the Faithful. The longer I remain in the dark, the tighter hope holds me. I've had time to sort things out in that dungeon you left me in. I know now this is how it's supposed to be. I am of both worlds, Sebastian." I stepped over Lucas so I was face to face with Sebastian. "But you already knew that, didn't you?"

I allowed him to reach down and take the sword from me. He walked over to the altar, put it down and lifted my sword, made of crystallized seawater and rock. It shined like a beacon, much like the pendant that hung from my neck. He turned the sword over in his hands a few times, admiring it, inspecting it. The box lay open on the altar. He closed it then walked toward me, stopping halfway between us.

"We seem to have hit a wall, Samantha. I cannot let Ethan go, you see. We haven't had time to properly catch up. He was certainly surprised to learn that dear old dad was the leader of the Exiled."

"So you told him?"

"I did. You knew?"

"I figured it out recently. His mother gave him up out of love and you killed her."

"I did. I couldn't find him for a long time. When I did, I saw that he was not the impressionable lad I had hoped for so I focused my attention on the one who was."

"Lucas."

"You are correct! Yes, my vulnerable nephew. He was eager enough, hungry enough, for the attention I offered that he hung on my every word. It wasn't hard. My brother and his wife were so focused on directing Ethan toward the Faithful, so focused on making sure he left all the darkness he was born into behind him, that they failed to spend the same time with their own son. They forgot that remaining Faithful is a choice. They never gave Lucas a reason to choose."

"And you did."

"Very perceptive. I just showed him all he could become under my...tutelage, shall we say? Every time he doubted my path, I was there to whisper in his ear. Every time he thought he loved you, I was there to point out what was simmering between you and Ethan. And that drove him closer to me. Before long, he grew to hate Ethan and all his righteous beliefs." He walked about me in circles, lazily touching my hair, my face as he did. "After all, Lucas was granted his wings. Where were Ethan's? How could Ethan be chosen as a guardian angel, let alone *your* guardian angel, if he hadn't even earned his wings yet? Had no one to grant them? Yes. It was easy. And that thin line humans speak of, the one between love and hate, all it took was the tiniest jiggle and Lucas leapt over it. He hates you, you know. Hates you almost as much as he hates Ethan. And it's the most delightful thing I've ever heard."

The anger that poured out of me all those times before was there and I was prepared to unleash it, but was held back by what my father told me: *Anger fueled by love will not condemn you. Anger in spite of love makes you no better than those you seek to destroy.* And I wanted to be better than Sebastian, better than those Exiled who took advantage of their position. There must be balance in order for peace to reign. There was a place for the Exiled. Just as there was a place for the Faithful. Sebastian failed to realize that. The Exiled needed us as much as the Faithful need them. The hard pill of reality didn't go down easy but there it was. By destroying all the hope in the word, the Exiled would eventually destroy themselves. A little fact Sebastian had kept for himself, I was sure.

"And my father? What about him? You killed him for something you can't destroy anyway."

He spoke carelessly, waving my question away like he was waving away a fly. "Ah, well. Casualty of war, I guess. He stood in the way of what I wanted, of what I needed, and he paid with his life. And for his father's betrayal. You should be happy. Faithful all over the world are celebrating him like a martyr. So don't be mad at *me*. I made him famous."

The dam holding me back cracked. My eyes were still round and black, my skin still hazed with shadow but something else pulsed behind it Sadness? That was new. It overwhelmed me. Not sadness for the fact that Sebastian killed my father but heartache for the fact that he was gone, period. The feeling was warm and uncomfortable. I fought to tamp it down but the crack widened.

I began to circle toward him and he mirrored me, knowing a fight was imminent.

"Do not talk about my father like you did him a favor. You took him from me. You took him away and I was never able to say goodbye. You can stand on your soapbox and preach about celebrity and favors and temptation but you have no clue why people hope. You can't take it away if you don't know where it comes from."

"Let me ask you a question, Samantha. Have
296

you seen yourself? Not just the evil monster growing inside you, but the outside you? Have you seen your transformation? Your skin, once golden hued and soft, now radiates shadows. Your once beautiful blue eyes are no longer. Once the color of a Tahitian ocean, they have become blacker than hate. Even your tears are stained with the raven-colored tinge of despair. Your transformation is irreversible, you know. Even I am having trouble recognizing the flighty teenager you once were. And it's hypnotic. Fueled by hate or love, hope or despair, you will not return to who you once were. And it's magnificent."

His words hit me and I realized he was right. I would never be the girl I was when this all began. Physically, I could tell the difference and I now knew everything about me had changed.

He took a few steps toward me, my sword still in his hand. "I think I have had enough of this conversation, my dear Samantha. Hand over the pendant."

"No."

He stopped mid-stride and grinned sarcastically. "No? Not this defiant conversation again, Samantha. You saw what happened the last time you told me no."

He closed the distance between us quickly and held his hands to my head. Forced to my knees, I

297

heard the roar of the ocean, the clash of swords, the cries of battle. I was back on the cliff. My eyes were commanded downward and I could do nothing but listen to the slaughter of Faithful and Exiled alike. My whole being was enraged with despair. Despair that both my Faithful brothers and sisters and my Exiled counterparts were fighting and dying over the whim of one.

"Now Samantha, please look around you. All this is your doing."

Jesse lay dead to my left, wings torn off. Mara collapsed in tears over the remains of Christian. Noah was in battle, still, with a faceless being that looked more like rotting wood than a person. Cal was the only one missing. The only sign left of him was half a wing and a sword that lay abandoned near the cliff's edge. I could only assume he'd been cast over. Lucas held Ethan's arms behind his back as Sebastian drove a sword through him.

"No! No!"

"I will make this happen, Samantha. They will all be dead and you will be at fault."

I fell into a huddle of painful anguish. I wailed and kicked and punched. *What had I done!* They were all dead or would soon be. All because of me. All because of the choices I had yet to make. The choices I'd been too scared to make.

Sebastian took over my head again as the scene switched to an unfamiliar alley. I could make out the shadow of what appeared to be a dumpster. A man kneeled before the dumpster, holding his arms to the sky and shouting something I couldn't understand. Behind him, a dark figure swooped in. The man stretched out his wings as the dark figure raised his sword. I screamed as I saw the figure drop his sword along the man's back and watched the crumpled wings fall silently to the damp pavement. In an instant, the figure knocked the man over and stood above him. I could hear the man's thoughts.

Samantha.

Sebastian was showing me my father's death. Everything in the vision became clear and saw my father's defiant face. I saw that he knew he was going to die and I could see triumph in his eyes.

The dark figure standing above my father was Sebastian, face grotesquely twisted. Hate poured from him as he slowly plunged the sword deep into my father's chest.

"Dad!"

Sebastian removed his hands from me and knelt down to search my eyes. He could see I was about to lose myself and he encouraged it. His hands caressed my hair in a way that made me ill and even though he could see the look of disgust cloud my face, he brushed his lips across my eyes.

Sebastian reveled in the pain of others, especially if the outcome suited him. He had laid down my sword in front of me, daring me to reach for it. I gingerly grasped it and slid it closer to me. The pendant began to glow brighter, again. Its heaviness had become cumbersome. With my eyes still downcast, a light caught the corner of my eye. My father stood behind Lucas.

Samantha, it is time. You must choose now. Choose your path. Whichever you choose will be hard. Your life is not meant to be easy. The war between the Exiled and the Faithful will see to that. Choose now. This battle is yours to win or lose.

"Lucas, No!"

I turned my head quickly at the sound of Ethan's voice. He wasn't dead! As the thought entered my head, I was knocked over from behind, my head singing from the blow. I quickly gathered my bearings and looked for my attacker. Lucas.

"Give up now, Sam. You won't win. Join us."

I stood, sword in hand, ready for the confrontation. "You don't want to do this, Lucas. Think about the past, think of your family, of Ethan…of me. You can't be so far gone that you would destroy us all."

I saw him waver a minute before Sebastian's

voice thundered.

"Destroy her now, Lucas! If she will not give us the Heart of Hope then we must kill her and take it for ourselves."

Lucas drew his sword high over his head and sent it crashing down. At the last minute I blocked his attack with my sword. The clash of our swords was deafening in the empty cavern of the room. The windows shook as Lucas and I fought and we became locked in a dance of skill. Determination set in his eyes. The force of his strikes increased with each blow. Darkness was fueling him.

"Lucas!" I yelled between defensive moves. "Don't listen to him. You don't want to do this. I know you don't."

"You know nothing. I will do what I have to. As long as you are alive and haven't joined with us, you are the enemy. I have chosen with whom I stand. You still waver and that makes you weak."

Inflexible resolve heightened within me, and adrenaline coursed through my blood. I could see it in his eyes. He was no longer the Lucas I grew up with. He'd become a dark monster. Sebastian had twisted his mind beyond repair. The choice I had to make was for the good of everyone, regardless of what side they were on. The Faithful must know they could not lazily jump ship and head for the temptation of the

Exiled. The Exiled must know they could not take advantage of their position in this world. All must be balanced and fair.

I twisted to the left and dropped to the floor as Lucas aimed his sword at my head. He kicked out and landed his foot in my gut, knocking the wind out of me. I moved to get up but it was too late. Lucas was standing above me, Sebastian just behind him with a look of gleeful hatred on his face. For a moment Lucas looked into my eyes and we connected. It was a connection of long lost friendship and love. It lasted mere seconds before his face twisted back into the demon he had become. With a forceful growl he dropped his sword downward, aimed at my neck.

Time slowed down as Lucas' sword came towards me. A blinding flash of light distracted everyone in the room and the winged girl from my dreams appeared between us and everything around me froze in time. I turned my head to take in her beauty. She cast a light so intense, almost like an eclipse and I felt like I might be blinded if I stared too long but I could do nothing to tear my gaze from her.

"Do what you must, Samantha. But know that from this day on, your actions will be remembered. Good or bad, people will know who you are. Both the Exiled and the Faithful will follow whatever foot you put forward. Do what it is you feel will balance the scales of darkness and light. A decision must be made."

Everything moved slowly. She faded and I saw Ethan stand. He limped toward Sebastian, with a sword in his hand. He was clutching his stomach and could barely keep himself upright but the look on his face told me all I needed to know. I used the moment of distraction the girl had provided me to roll away from the tip of Lucas' sword. Everything moved quickly now and as I leapt to my feet behind Lucas, I heard Sebastian gasp as I brought my sword down and stripped Lucas of his wings. With a terrible wail, Lucas fell to the floor, his sword clattering out of his reach. Instantly, Sebastian stood before me, his demonic features fully exposed. His face was so frightening; I wanted to look away but forced myself to stand firm.

"What have you done?" He shrieked; all trace of composure eliminated. He threw me across the room.

Standing, I wiped blood from my mouth as I replied defiantly, "I've done what needed to be done."

"Then why don't you finish him?" His words taunted me. His hatred intensified to a manic state. He had lost all control. He knew his plans were unraveling, as I refused to play into his hand.

"His death would have been needless.

Because his choices were not fully his own, his death would be senseless. Without his wings, he'll be less of a threat. If he is to continue serving you, then he will do it without his wings for now. They'll heal slowly and painfully; you should find joy in that Sebastian. Lucas was lost and you took advantage of his impressionable nature. For that, he need not be punished."

"You show mercy after his betrayal? After he told me where your father would be? After he used you and turned against you? For his sins, you show mercy?" His tone was baffled and aggressive.

"Yes. And I will do the same to any Exiled interested in disturbing the symmetry of humanity. Mine is not a path of destruction but of equilibrium. If the scales are tipped, I will right them. That is the mercy I show. That is the balance I bring, the path I walk."

"He will come back stronger. I will see to it."

Sebastian raised his arms above his head and I was lifted off my feet and dropped furiously to the ground but still I forced myself to stand back up and face him.

"I killed your father and I will kill you. When I destroy the Heart of Hope and the Box of Hope, darkness will extend to every corner of this world and into the next. You have not beaten me."

"I will fight you to my last breath, Sebastian. You will not win. Not as long as I am breathing."

He screamed. "You cannot kill me."

"Not now I can't. Just as you cannot kill me."

He looked to Ethan, who was standing behind me, sword drawn. Bruised and damaged, determination outlined his face. Blood dripped from his neck where Lucas had tried to behead him but failed. The thought riled malevolence to the surface and I fought to push it back down.

Sebastian pleaded with Ethan. "My son. Come back to me. I will right the wrongs I have done to you and together we will rule as equals."

"You aren't my father," Ethan's voice was hoarse.

"I am. And inside you can feel it. You can feel the darkness struggling to get out, to make amends with the father you shun. You and I are meant to own this world. You are my blood and I am yours. Come back and together we will triumph."

"I won't join you, Sebastian. You stopped being my father the day you killed my mother. Samantha is who I follow. She is the one chosen by both light and dark, by the stories of both Exiled and Faithful. She has my allegiance. Not you. I will never follow you."

My pendant's incandescent light burned a hole

in my chest but I refused to flinch. My face reflected back to me through Sebastian's dilated eyes and I understood fully that my transformation was permanent. I still looked like me, only different. My skin had taken on a porcelain glow, much like that of the angel that visited me in my dreams. My eyes were still round and black and oily tears stained my otherwise angelic face.

Behind me I could make out the faint shadow of something out of place. A shimmering image of black and silver reflected what little light streamed through the stained glass. I closed my eyes and concentrated as my wings unfurled for the first time. Sebastian's eyes widened from the slits they'd become and I could see his fear for the first time.

"Then you will suffer the same fate at your precious *Samantha*. This isn't over," he yelled as he stepped back from me. "You will not defeat me. I will rule this world. I will destroy whatever humanity is left and all will kneel before me."

"That will never happen, Sebastian." My voice was quiet and steady. My wings pulled back and beat forward with a force that sent Sebastian flying against the altar, knocking the box to the ground.

"You bitch!" The pitch and tone of his voice shattered the stained glass windows above and crumbled the foundation of the room. I beat my wings again and Sebastian fell with a generous crash that would have killed a mortal. Blood spilled from his head, though I could already see him beginning to heal. Walls cracked and a chasm opened in the middle of the floor. Animal-like, Sebastian crawled, wings spread out for cover, over to Lucas with the box securely in his hands. Ethan and I stood, now side by side, watching him cower away. He dragged Lucas' limp body across the floor toward the rupture. Ethan moved to stop him but I held out my hand gently to hold him back. He didn't question me, instead he held his sword at his side, his eyes fixed on his brother.

"Let him go, Ethan."

"Will he ever come back to us?" he asked quietly.

"No. He's gone, for now. He'll be back, and I fear he'll be stronger. Sebastian will make it so. Until then, let him go."

The roof began to cave bit by bit but still we stood, watching and waiting for Sebastian to take Lucas away. At the edge of the split, Sebastian looked at us with turbulent madness.

"I will kill you both." In a hazy mist of shadow, Lucas, Sebastian and the Box of Hope fell into the darkness.

Epilogue

Torn, damaged and weary, Ethan and I returned to the house that once belonged to Jesse. The idea that it was our home now wasn't lost on me. This was where we would now eat our meals, rest our heads, heal, and plan for the future. The others – Christian, Mara, Branna, Cal and Noah – were waiting for us when we walked through the door. Branna rushed over and hugged Ethan.

"I am so sorry Ethan. None of us had any idea about Lucas. Is it true he now follows Sebastian?"

Stepping away from her, his reply was hoarse and filled with sadness. "It's true. He has been for a while now. He's the one who gave Sebastian James' location."

"No! I don't believe it!" Cal growled. "He loved James as much as any of us. He stood in for him to train her and now he follows the Exiled?"

He pointed his finger at me and I instantly bristled. Once again my anger vibrated through the air around me but I was able to tamp it down even when dark tears slid down my face. "I don't want to believe it either. I've known him my whole life. Sebastian has twisted his head. Brainwashed him, if you will. I'm not sure he can be saved but I intend to try."

"But look at you! Shadows live within you. Just look at your eyes, your skin. You've changed."

"This is who I am. I am the balance between light and dark. And I wasn't able to do much damage to Sebastian until I let the darkness all the way in and used it against him."

Noah stepped forward and asked the question I knew was on everyone's mind. "Why didn't you kill Sebastian?"

"I couldn't."

"Why? And why didn't he kill Ethan? Or Lucas? Or you for that matter?" He threw his hands up in exasperation.

"I don't know all the answers and the ones I do have can wait. For now, Ethan and I – all of us, need to rest. This isn't over. Sebastian made that very clear. He still has the Box of Hope and I still have the pendant. I'm going to need you, all of you."

Noah sat with his head in his hands. "Where else am I going to go?"

Mara stood. "I'll stand with you, Samantha."

They seemed able to put past distrust aside and stand with me. Together, we mourned the death of our friends and loved ones as well as the betrayal of a friend and brother. Together, we waited for

Sebastian and planned for his return.

None of them had ever confronted Sebastian. Ethan and I were the only ones who had not only stood before him, but had lived long enough to tell about it. It was what kept the others close to me. The youngest and, by far, the least familiar with all of this, I became their leader. The one they looked to for guidance and training. They knew we would meet with Sebastian again. And I knew Lucas would be standing at his side. I would do what I could to shield them from the wrath that was sure to come but they had to be prepared if I was unable.

The memory of that day followed us relentlessly - Lucas' betrayal, Jesse's death, Sebastian's vow to return. My father's cryptic messages had dropped me into the path of my fate. I did not know why I was chosen and I still mourned my blue eyes, wingless back, best friend, and normalcy. That, however, was no longer a life for me. Everything I once held dear, everything I once took for granted, had vanished into mere remembrance. Thoughts and memories that were once rigid and firm became pliable, moldable. Snapshots of who I once was would eventually fade into nothing. Until then, I kept them close.

Ethan had taken his place beside me to ensure I remained balanced. Whereas I was filled with darkness, he was filled with light. When I was overcome with thoughts of despair, he counteracted with faith and hope. When he could not handle the pain and suffering, I took it from him. And that pain usually came to him at night, in his dreams. The betrayal of his brother was too much for him to take though it did not push him toward the ways of the Exiled. In fact, if anything, he held onto the Faithful with a tighter grip.

The bond between us deepened. What lay ahead for us was still a mystery. Could he and I, in spite of all that had happened, make something of our feelings for each other? And even more important, should we? Those questions remained to be answered so for now, I tightened my grip around the lingering shadow of his kiss and the warmth of his touch.

The balance between light and dark, hope and despair rested on my shoulders. What began as training exercises designed to keep me from falling into Sebastian's grasp turned into my metamorphosis. Instead of rejecting darkness, I allowed it to consume me. With it and the light of hope, I would walk the line between both worlds. This was a burden my father hoped would not fall to me. I was the personification of legend and myth; a whispered story passed from Faithful to Faithful and from Exiled to Exiled. Both stood with the knowledge that there could not be hope without despair, light without dark, life without death. They looked to me, for better or worse. Here on earth, the fallen angels have been charged to me.

And I must try to save them all.

Even Lucas.

END BOOK I

Chapter 1

Ethan was bound and determined to keep my training schedule. Up at the crack of dawn, we trekked out, once again into the woods. Ever since his brother betrayed the both of us by siding with Sebastian, we didn't speak during our training sessions. Not out loud anyway. At least not until that morning.

I want you to come at me with all you've got.

Ethan, how many times can we do this? I'm tired.

We can't quit, Sam. Sebastian is going to come back. He is going to come for you. Now pick up that rock and throw it at me.

Resigned to do what he asked, I flattened my hand towards the ground and concentrated on lifting the rock so it floated in front of me. His eyes narrowed as it began to spin in front of me. My eyes on his, I concentrated in pushing all my power to the rock. I began to float it from one hand to the other.

You're stalling.

Immediately the rock lifted into palm and I threw it with everything I had. He was able to duck and catch it and before I knew what was happening, it hit me square in the nose.

"What the fuck, Ethan?" Blood oozed through my fingers. The sky darkened with my pain.

"You're supposed to pay attention."

"I was paying attention. Shit." Pulling my shirt up to my face, I tried to wipe away the blood. The pain was already subsiding and I knew, even if my nose was broken, it was already beginning to heal.

"Let me look." Ethan stomped over; his annoyance was more than obvious.

"No. It's fine."

"No, it's not fine, Samantha. You weren't paying attention. You always have to pay attention."

"Jesus, relax."

"I will not fucking relax. This is what I'm talking about. You can't get lazy, you can't *relax*. Sebastian will come back." He picked up a rock and crushed it in his hand.

"You don't think I know that? You don't think I, of all freaking people, know that?"

"You aren't the only one who's lost in all this." His words barely floated above a whisper as he walked away.

I moved toward him and placed my hand on his shoulder. "I know. We'll get Lucas back."

"I don't think we will, Sam. He's gone." He put his hands to his head and screamed, "Fuck!"

"Ethan calm down. Let's start over. Come on. I'll throw the rock."

He spun and grabbed my face. "You don't get it. I won't lose you to Sebastian like I lost my brother, like you lost your father. I won't let it happen. I'd do anything to keep you safe." His shoulders dropped. "I just wish you'd work a little harder. Help me out here."

"Ethan…"

He held up his hands. "No. Forget it. That's enough training for today. We'll do it again tomorrow."

I waited until I couldn't see him anymore before I turned and walked toward the cliff. All I wanted was peace.

Distracted, I picked the lint off my jeans and stared out into the water. My playlist on low, I let Of Monsters and Men fill me with words of love, love, love – *Sure, if I even knew what that was anymore.* As the sun continued to rise on the morning, my eyes darted impatiently. The music didn't have its usual calming effect on me. If anything, I was getting more wired by the minute and I rubbed the back of my neck to relieve some of the tension. Goosebumps came and went, darkness faded in and out and I was sure something was coming. But I didn't retreat. It was only there that I didn't need to be strong, that I could let go and try to be me. Whoever that was anymore.

Sitting on the edge of the cliff where Jesse died, where I'd found out Lucas had betrayed me, often brought me comfort when I couldn't quell the storm in my head. Legs dangling over the side, I allowed my wings to spread beside me. Swirls of black and silver cast shadows while reflecting the light. The image reflected who I'd become. Their heaviness had lightened over the past few weeks and my shoulders didn't hurt as much. I ran my hand over the soft feathers as I contemplated everything I wasn't.

Once blue, the eyes that stared back at me in the mirror were coal black and my skin, once sun-kissed took on the hue of a porcelain doll. But, despite the wings and other changes, my new physical self was nothing compared to what'd happened to me inside. I was no longer the same carefree teenager, either. The only thing that worried be back then was what to wear to school. Now my heart, my head, and my soul were torn between good and evil. It should've been an easy enough choice. Unfortunately, because of all the mess and fighting and betrayal, my life was no longer easy. I was one temper tantrum away from transforming completely into an Exiled.

My father was once an Exiled who chose to join the Faithful. Instead of reveling in sins, he fought for forgiveness. Instead of whining and moaning of events that occurred out of his control, he chose to do what was right. Not what was easiest. And that's where I struggled most. I didn't know if I was strong enough for all of it. And more often than not, I wanted to give in to all the temptations and live with the ease of the Exiled. The only thing that kept me from joining Sebastian and his followers was the small piece of my heart, the part only Ethan could find, that reminded me of who I was meant to be. Balance. I must fight the Exiled with the darkness that flowed through me. And I must lead the Faithful with the light that pulsed inside my heart. Somehow, I needed to make sure they both lived in harmony. After all, what would there be to hope for if there was nothing to despair?

Sebastian's voice hadn't invaded since I saw Lucas and him fall through the earth though I knew he was watching, waiting. He vowed to return and I had no reason to doubt his words. The problem was, I didn't know when or where he and I would come face to face again.

As I sat ruminating the past and contemplating my future, the heart shaped opal pendant that hung from my neck, the Heart of Hope, began to glow and my skin began to burn beneath it. As long as I wore it, I knew Sebastian could find me. And part of me hoped he would. The part that hoped all this would finally be done. My hand fisted around the sword that lay beside me. Every muscle in my body tensed as I concentrated on finding the source of evil that had invaded my space. My skin tingled a warning and the hairs on the back of my neck stood and my feathers ruffled as I moved into a crouch as I heard a soft footfall upon the morning frost giveaway the intruder. I silently called for Ethan and hoped that he'd hear me. So often the past few weeks, he was nowhere to be found.

When I whirled around, sword drawn in front of me, the tip of it grazed the chin of one of them. An Exiled. Body oddly contorted with bony wings and a slim sharp sword pointed directly at my heart, it smiled and bared its ugly yellow teeth. *Repulsive.*

"Samantha."

"What do you want?" Anger pulsed as the air around me grew electric and the sea below riled up in response.

"Please, lower your weapon. I am not here to harm you. I am here to deliver a message." Its voice pierced my ears like nails on a chalkboard.

"I'm pretty sure I asked you a question. Who are you?" I gripped the handle of my ever-present sword tighter.

"I am Malakai. I have a message for the one who maintains balance."

"Well, you found her. And her name is Samantha. What's your message?" I pictured driving my sword through its heart and removing its wings. Slowly. The image wasn't as disturbing as it should have been.

"Sam!"

I faltered a moment at the sound of Ethan's voice. *Oh, thank God.* I wasn't quite used to the fact that he knew when I was filling with darkness even if it seemed as though he was avoiding me lately. I hated the fact that even though I loved him we could never be together because he was my guardian angel. *Angels and their stupid rules.*

"Ethan. I'm here."

Malakai's smile grew grotesquely wider and thick saliva dripped from his teeth. His paper-thin wings spread out beside him, readying for a fight.

Ethan entered the clearing, sword drawn and pointed at my visitor.

"I am to deliver the message to only you, Samantha. Beg him leave." Malakai spoke.

"No. You don't call the shots. You will deliver whatever message you need to deliver then get the hell out of here or Ethan will slice off your wings and I will drive my sword through that thing you call a heart."

His eyes surveyed the situation. With Ethan at his back and me standing in front of him, Malakai must've quickly figured out that I didn't deal out idle threats. And I was sure the fact that I was barely clinging to whatever control I had left didn't escape him. As shadows invaded the space and swirled around me, he lowered his sword to his side, folded his wings and bowed his head slightly. "Very well."

Feeling sufficiently badass, I nodded to Ethan and he took a few steps back lowering his sword slightly and I did the same as my eyes darted around, quickly surveying the area for more of them. I was once again struck with the odd notion that the connection he and I have shared since this all started was somehow broken. A low buzz reverberated in my head. *Shake it off, Sam.*

It was hard tamping down the growing need to kill Malakai. I hated that feeling. Ethan's presence was the only thing keeping me centered. "Speak."

"I have news. Sebastian is planning an attack. Lucas is healing at a slower rate than expected and Sebastian isn't pleased. He is focused on killing you.

Killing both of you." His eyes shifted toward Ethan. "He has a plan."

"What's this plan?" Ethan's voice was firm.

"I am not privy to that information. I am not in his circle."

"You've come to tell me that?" Annoyance dripped from my words. "You come to me promising a message and you do nothing more than tell us what we already know? I think it's time for you to leave. Ethan." Our swords rose once again.

"Lucas isn't healing as quickly as Sebastian would like. That much I know."

"You already said that. What do you know about Lucas?"

"Sebastian is very angry with him."

I snorted. "I'm sure."

Malakai cocked his grotesque head to the side. "His betrayal is the only thing you focus on?"

"It's the only thing I can focus on." Rage built up and threatened to break free.

Ethan stepped closer, the tip of his sword grazing the back of Malakai. Eyes wide, he replied hastily. "You haven't let me finish. I do have a message from one who is in Sebastian's circle. One you've never met but have heard about. One who is tired of Sebastian's ways. One who wants to return to how it's supposed to be."

"And who is the 'one' you speak of?"

"He is the one who has sent me to deliver his message."

Vibrations ran through me. "Stop talking in circles! Give the message you were sent to give or I will kill you. You have no place here."

"Ahh." Malakai's eyes narrowed. "I told him you wouldn't listen. I told him you were not ready to hear his proposal. You are still…immature."

"Enough!" The tip of Ethan's sword pierced the wing of the Exiled. "Go back to whoever sent you. Tell them we don't talk in circles. If you have nothing to tell us, we have nothing to listen to. Our patience is wearing thin."

Malakai's hands flew to his face as he began to shake. Didn't really look to me like whoever had sent him had thought any it through. This minion was about to crack under the pressure. I was only too happy to speed up that process.

Arms outstretched, he stepped away. "No. No. I was sent. You must listen. Death at your hand would be welcomed in light of what I will face if I fail. You must listen. The purest fallen has sent me. He is ready to make a deal with you to overthrow Sebastian and rid the world of him once and for all."

My mind raced as I tried to process the information. *Who was the purest fallen?*

Ethan whispered and I barely hear him over the din that began to rise around me. "Damien."

Acknowledgements

This book wouldn't have been possible without few wonderful people. First, I would like to thank my husband for his constant love and support. His confidence in me gave me to boost I needed to start this journey. I love you very much, Jim. Additionally, my family has been so supportive of this endeavor. Each and every one of you gets a huge "thank you" for believing in me, especially my two boys.

Next, I'd like to thank Cyn Balog for her encouragement. Thank you for showing me how to be an "I did."

I'd also like to thank SJ Davis and everyone at Crushing Hearts and Black Butterfly Publishing for believing in this story as much as I do.

A big "thank you" goes out to Katherine Hughes who was the first person to read the book in its entirety.

Thank you to Michelle Johnson for suggesting I submit to CHBB, Sarah Carr for putting in a good word and Pyxi Rose for being so supportive.

To Leslie Wright – just because you are awesome.

To Rue Volley for creating the most beautiful cover, thank you so much. You are amazing!

And finally, I'd like to thank my new friends at CHBB. I'm so happy TORN has a new home.